PRAISE FOR *TANGLED ROOTS*

"I'd definitely recommend this read to fellow PNR-loving readers who are looking for something out with the norm (even for PNR!). An enchanting start to a new series by a new-to-me-author!"
~ *Tangents & Tissues*

"Fast-paced, mysterious, enthralling, gripping, magical, exciting, and romantic…I haven't read many witchy books, but *Tangled Roots* was everything I imagined those books would be."
~ *Bibliomedico*

"Witches. Spells. Love. A magical modern day Sleeping Beauty story if Aurora was part of a witch's coven."
~ *Nurse Bookie Book Blog*

"This is a well written, enthralling story that I thoroughly enjoyed escaping into. The character development is great, bringing them to life in the pages of the story…a fast paced, magical mystery with plenty of intrigue, suspense and surprises."
~ *Little Mrs Reader*

TANGLED FATES

TANGLED MAGIC SERIES: BOOK 2
DENISE D. YOUNG

Text copyright © 2020 by Denise D. Young.
Published by Sage & Shadows Books.
All rights reserved.

"Come to the Labyrinth" lyrics copyright 2007 by S. J. Tucker. Quotation used with artist's permission.

eISBN: 978-0-9980756-4-8
print ISBN: 978-0-9980756-5-5

Cover Design by Victoria Cooper Art
Editing by Critiques by Katie
Proofreading by Erin Zarro

Sage & Shadows Books

DEDICATION

To all those brave souls who've started down the well-trodden path, listened to their hearts, and turned away, charting their own course. I hope you find wildness, magic, love, and belonging on your journey.
I know I have on mine.

Blessed Be.

"It only takes the tiniest of fires sometimes
to light the way you knew was always there.
In the heart of matters, it's the journey keeps us warm,
the lights that lead us where we are to go.
May you raise your eyes and know with every step:
we are not alone."

"COME TO THE LABYRINTH"
S. J. TUCKER

PROLOGUE

Aiden
Two Years Ago

The earth sang its magic beneath my paws tonight. The moon was full, the September sky clear, a smattering of stars like glitter spilled against black paper.

In my fox form, I slinked through the forests that edged my family's estate. We weren't technically supposed to shift here—one of my father's many rules—but who would know? I was home from law school for the weekend, and my fox needed a moonlit adventure even more than usual. So, here I was.

My family's estate, just outside of Savannah, Georgia, spanned sixty acres, much of it wooded, the sprawling Greek Revival-style home surrounded by magnolias and boxwoods.

I caught a strange scent. The ley lines of the earth tugged on me, the way a compass's magnet points the traveler home. I perked my ears, waiting for whatever creature drew my fox's attention.

Nothing. I caught the scent of a rabbit nearby, and the hoot of an owl in a nearby oak. But mostly, besides the normal woodland beasties, I was alone.

No. That tug again, pulling me forward, toward the City of Savannah and the Atlantic Ocean.

I closed my eyes.

Ah. It wasn't a physical sensation then, but a mystical one, some powerful magical force.

The scent of violets, moss, and candlewax drifted toward me. I sighed and stepped forward, drawn, ineffably, toward that intoxicating aroma of magic.

Peaceful and wild. My nerve endings were electrified, yet my spirit quieted. That energy... It felt like witchcraft mingled with something far more ancient.

I crept forward, my body, blanketed in coppery fur, low against the earth. A lone cloud slid across the moon, shielding me as I entered the space between the woods and the expansive gardens behind my parents' home.

Magical energy skittered over my skin, like fingertips sliding down my back.

Could foxes purr? Because I was purring right now.

If the woman who created that energy were here right now, I was pretty sure I'd roll over and let her rub my belly. I felt certain she was a witch—only a witch could create such a wake of magical energy. I felt equally certain that whoever she was, she was miles away—in Savannah, perhaps, or on a nearby beach.

I lay down, letting the magic sing against my skin. My body sunk into the earth, heavy and warm.

Whoever she was, she felt like home. Not this home, full of Waterford crystal and artwork that cost more than most people's cars.

Just...home.

"Wake up, you idiot!" A foot kicking me in the side woke me up. I stirred. My brother, Liam, thirteen months my junior, stood over me, scowling in the moonlight.

"Huh?" I wiped drool off my mouth with the back of my hand.

My hand? I jumped up. "Shit!" I'd fallen asleep and, in my sleep, shifted back into my human form.

Liam's scowl deepened. He held out a navy-blue bathrobe. "Go upstairs and get dressed. Family meeting in Dad's study in five minutes."

I shrugged into the bathrobe, curse words like galloping horses thudding in my brain.

Liam stood on his tiptoes to match my height. Right in my face, he growled, "Five. Minutes."

I couldn't help but take a step backward. I tried to hide it by making a show of adjusting the belt of my robe, but Liam sniffed, the wolf shifter in the family seeming pleased he'd managed to make his big brother submit, even for half a second.

He strode away, and I rushed inside and up the back staircase to my room.

I'd broken more than my share of rules over the years but shifting on the estate was strictly forbidden.

And falling asleep in the grass, in view of the house while Liam's non-magical fiancée was visiting?

That was one line no one dared cross.

I slinked into the study seven minutes later.

"You're late," Dad growled without turning away from the expansive windows overlooking the immaculately groomed gardens.

Mom fussed nervously with her hair, and Liam spun the oversized globe beside Dad's desk in what I knew was a false display of casualness. My brother was more afraid of our father than I was.

My father turned slowly away from the window, a towering six-foot-three, close-cropped salt-and-pepper hair, a neatly trimmed beard. Even at this late hour, his crisp white button-down and black trousers appeared newly pressed. His lips turned into a snarl. Even decades of potions that suppressed his shifter magic couldn't completely quell the wolf lurking within.

My inner fox whimpered—he knew a superior predator when he saw one. And I, the son who often toed the line, sometimes crossed it, but eventually remembered his place, cowered.

My dad crossed the room. We were the same height in sheer inches, but in presence he dwarfed me the way he dwarfed rival lawyers in the courtroom.

"George Washington himself would cower in my presence," he once told me. I was thirteen. I'd just shifted for the first time—the first fox shifter in a century in our bloodline.

Bile rose in my throat. His magic might be long suppressed, but my father didn't need magic to be ruthless. I forced myself to stand my ground.

My father scowled. "Your brother's fiancée saw you out in the garden."

Oh, hell. "Bianca saw me shift?"

Liam stepped forward. "She saw you napping—naked."

"Let's be thankful that's all she saw," my father growled, shooting Liam a look. My brother stepped backward, fading into the polished mahogany woodwork.

My father walked over to the large globe in its brass stand, a pale ivory with deep brown outlines for continents and scrolled lettering. He flipped it open to reveal his potions stash. He plucked out a crimson red vial with a black stopper.

"I've given you almost a decade to make this decision on your own. I've waited through all of your foolishness. You're a grown man now. You'll be a lawyer in a few years. It's time to stop acting like a child."

I stepped backward, toward the door. "You promised it would be my decision."

"Your carelessness tonight shows you don't have the guts or the sense to do what's necessary."

"It wasn't like that." What could I say? I sensed an alluring magic, and its lullaby sang my fox to sleep? Even to me, it sounded ridiculous. To my father, who regarded such whimsical magicks as the greatest of follies?

No. In my family's eyes, there was no defense.

I glanced at my mother, but she was studying the oil painting of my grandfather that hung on the wall. Liam was staring at the antique rug as if it held the secrets of the universe.

I was alone in this.

"No."

"You've forfeited your choice, Aiden," my father growled.

"You can't force me to take some damn potion I don't want to take."

My father glanced at my brother. "Now, Liam."

With the swiftness of twin wolves leaping on a stunned antelope, they pinned me to the wall. I fought, thrashing, kicking, but it was two against one, and I was no match for the two of them.

My mother, up to this point silent, took the vial from my father and unstoppered it. "Your father assures me you'll get used to the taste." She said it with the saccharine sweetness of a mother trying to get a small child to take his cough medicine.

I clenched my jaw, but with surprising strength, she pried my mouth open, tilted my chin up, and forced the liquid down my throat, holding my nose to force me to swallow it.

It tasted like swamp water, and I gagged. After I'd swallowed it, Liam and my father released me.

I staggered from the room and fumbled my way, half-blind with pain, upstairs. Spots danced in my vision, heart racing as the potion began to take effect. Why would anyone choose this madness, their magic curdling inside of them, their animal-self crying in pain, over the freedom of shifter magic?

I ran my hand along the toile wallpaper as I stumbled to the nearest bathroom. I vomited until the foul stuff was out of my system.

Inside me, my fox whimpered as if injured. Dark tendrils of magic floated in my vision, shadows hissing like some poisoned lullaby.

Not like the sweet song from earlier tonight, the one that sang of moon magic, white witchery, love and peace.

This? This was a darkness that threatened to consume my soul.

Run, my inner shifter whispered.

When the time is right, we run.

"I...Will," I slurred, my heart pounding an irregular rhythm.

I will.

CHAPTER ONE

Vivienne
Present Day: Midnight

The electric kettle beeped. I poured the steaming water over the cup of tea, my own unique blend of herbs and spices with decaf black tea leaves. The scents of cinnamon, bergamot, a bit of burdock root, and a dash of lemon peel rose up.

Outside, a fierce summer storm raged on. It would get worse before it got better.

It always got worse.

And no, I didn't mean the storm.

A loud *mew* interrupted my midnight crisis.

"Rosemary Caterwaul Broomsticks Gearhart, don't take that tone with me."

I pulled the cream out of the refrigerator and poured a splash into my cat's tiny lavender saucer, a find on my latest thrifting excursion with my friend Bailee. I stroked Rosemary's brindled fur. My beloved tortoiseshell cat, with her missing ear and crooked tail, was the first friend

I'd made when I came to Willow Creek shortly after Imbolc, the holiday we witches celebrated in February.

Bailee was the second.

To say a lot had happened in my six-month tenure in Willow Creek, Virginia, would be an understatement.

I poured a splash of cream into my tea, swirling the tea ball. I added a touch more honey than was necessary to satisfy my inner sweet tooth and stared into the darkening mug.

"Green Witch," the saying on the outside of the mug read, the deep-purple cursive script framed by an emerald green vine.

Bailee always smirked when she saw it. "It suits you," she always said with a knowing smile.

Now I was part of a makeshift coven of witches that included my Great-Aunt Cassie, who'd spent decades trapped in an oak tree, only to emerge still twenty years old and thinking it was 1974. Cassie's swoon-worthy boyfriend, Nick, also a witch; me; and my friend Bailee, the local librarian, rounded out the group.

A chirp from my phone indicated a text message. Rosemary cocked her head ever so slightly, acknowledging the sound but not stopping her dainty licking of cream from her saucer.

"I don't know who would be texting at this hour either," I told her. Not exactly true—I had an inkling.

I leaned against the counter in my tiny apartment kitchen. A gust of wind slammed against the brick building. It wasn't just a standard-issue July thunderstorm in the mountains.

There was dark magic awakening in Willow Creek. The storm was the earth's way of trying to wash it away.

"What's wrong?" the text message from Cassie read. I didn't bother to ask how Cassie knew. She just kind of *knew* things.

"Nothing. Can't sleep," I typed back. I sipped my tea. "Go to sleep," I typed, adding an animated GIF of someone sleeping to drive home the point. For a woman who'd never seen a cell phone until a week ago, Cassie learned quickly. To say she was enthusiastic about embracing everything the twenty-first century had to offer would be an understatement. She said she thought she belonged in the twenty-first century, more, perhaps, than she had in her own era.

"Can't," she messaged.

"Evan?" Ever since Cassie and Nick had gone to the Crossroads of Magic and returned with Nick's twin brother, their lives had been topsy-turvy. Evan was...terrified. Waves of pure fear radiated off the guy, as though decades of suffering and pain were trapped within him.

"Yes."

There was a pause, but I knew more was coming.

"Tell me what you need," I typed.

"That tea you make? ;)"

I ignored the winking smiley face. Cassie hadn't quite mastered the art of the emoji, and I'd leave it to Nick to explain them.

"Sure. Be right there."

I grabbed my go-to tote bag—black with a vintage print of red and pink cabbage roses on it—and tucked a few mason jars of my tea blends inside, along with a jar of local honey. I grabbed the small wooden box that contained my go-to crystals and slid that inside too.

"Sorry, Miss Rosemary. Magic calls." I let my fingers slide once more through her dark fur. She arched against my hand, her purr going full blast. "Sleep tight, lovely lady," I crooned. "One of us should get some rest."

She was circling in her pink cat bed by the window, searching for the comfiest position possible, when I shut the door behind me.

I ran, head down, through the rain. A brilliant flash of lightning lit up the night sky, followed by thunder so loud the ground beneath my feet seemed to tremble with it. I hit the unlock button on my key fob and practically dove into the driver's seat.

My hand flew automatically to the crystal at my neck. I rarely took off my rose quartz—only to regularly cleanse the cherished pink crystal with sage or when I was showering. Besides that, the stone was a constant presence at my throat. Sometimes I wore it on a long silver chain. Other times, on a velvet choker around my neck. Sometimes I'd pair it with other stones—amethyst and lapis lazuli were my favorites—if I needed the boost. Tonight, I wore smoky quartz. Some part of me needed the purifying, protective energy of the dark gray stone.

I started up the car and connected my phone to my car's sound system. I turned on my favorite playlist loud enough to hear above the rain. A selection of my favorite witchy tunes drowned out the storm as I drove.

The rose quartz, usually cool, was hot against my chest tonight.

I'd only driven to the Saunders Family Farm—Nick's family farm—a couple times, but I'd been blessed with an innate sense of direction. I navigated the mountain roads of Willow Creek like I'd been doing it my whole life and found a sort of pleasant ease. Bailee theorized it was a past-life memory. I figured I just had a good sense of direction.

I was halfway down Chestnut Hollow Lane, heading

toward the farm, now humming along to "May the Circle Be Open." The rain had stopped, leaving in its wake a low mist that clung to the wet ground.

Movement in the swathe of my headlights caught my eye. Instinctively, I hit the brakes before I registered what I was seeing.

I opened my mouth to scream as the car slammed to a stop, but no sound came out.

I clenched and unclenched my hands on the steering wheel.

With a screech of talons and a flurry of cream and brown feathers, the owl that had been flying straight at my car landed on the hood.

And stared at me.

I just stared back.

"Hi?" I croaked.

Yeah, crazy person. I shook my head. It was one thing to talk to my cat. But an owl?

The owl studied me with dark eyes, so brown they were almost black.

The cry she let loose was soft and pained.

She cried again, a soft, drawn-out series of hoots and hoos.

The owl tilted her head, her eyes like twin memories of shadow, deep with knowing. My fire magic sang under my skin, filling me with warmth.

She gave one last *hoo* and, with a stretching and rustling of her wings, alighted, disappearing into the misty night.

"From out of mist are wild things born.
Seek the truth beyond the thorn.
Where curses lurk and kin reside,
Fox and fire stem the tide."

The words tumbled from my mouth. I hadn't a clue what they meant, but I fumbled around inside my tote bag until I found a scrap of paper and a pen and scrawled them down.

The back porch light was on when I finally pulled into the driveway at the farm. I didn't even have to knock. Nick just swung the back door open and gestured me inside.

"Thanks for coming." He raked hand through mussed, shaggy blond hair, looking haggard. And why shouldn't he? His mother, grandmother, and other coven members were being held captive on some magical plane by his father, whom he'd just learned was an evil mastermind bent on destroying the magic of Willow Creek. He'd rescued his brother, only to find him a haunted shell of himself and...well, of course the guy looked exhausted.

"You okay?"

He shrugged. "Yeah. Cassie said you couldn't sleep so you were bringing some more of that tea. We wouldn't bother you, but we used up the last of the other batch, and it seems to help Evan sleep better."

I set my bag on the kitchen island. The farmhouse, even at nighttime, had a sunny, happy energy to it.

Sanctuary. That was the first thing I thought as I crossed the threshold. This house was a sanctuary for magic-workers. For witches. Like me. Like Nick. Like Cassie.

Cassie came around the corner, wearing a knee-length nightgown, ivory cotton trimmed in teal lace. Her look always seemed so vintage yet timeless at the same time — and that was Cassie, to a *T*, I was quickly learning.

She enveloped me in a quick hug, then stepped back.

"You had an adventure," she said. Again, she just *knew*.

"Owl," I supplied.

Cassie quirked an eyebrow as I handed her the mason jar of tea, a calming, grounding blend I'd come up with. "Oh?"

"Yeah." There was a plate of homemade gingersnaps on the island, and I helped myself to one, unable to resist anything with that combination of sugar and spice. "I'll have to go get some buffing compound tomorrow at the auto parts place, see if I can't get the scratches out."

Cassie set the mason jar on the island with a thud. "You hit it?"

"No," I quickly reassured her. "It—she, I'm pretty sure—landed on the hood of my car, gave me her message, then flew away."

"Was it a barred owl?" Nick asked as he filled the tea kettle and turned on the stove.

"I don't know. Not really an expert in birds of prey, Saint Nick."

I tried out the nickname Bailee often used when referring to her childhood friend. It didn't quite suit him—he wasn't really a jovial person, far more serious. Bailee said it was because Nick always tried to be perfect—you know, saintly, she said.

He pulled an image up on his phone.

"That's it." I grabbed another cookie. "Why?" I asked, brushing crumbs off my t-shirt. "Is that significant?"

Nick exhaled sharply. "The barred owl is the Guardian's familiar."

"The Guardian? Of the magic of Willow Creek?" I sucked in a breath. Oh, boy. What did the Guardian want with me? I knew she was the one who'd trapped Aunt Cassie in that tree back in the seventies. And now the

Guardian—a powerful, immortal being—was being held captive by Nick and Evan's father. So, a telepathic message from an owl when shadowy magic threatened Willow Creek was probably not a coincidence.

A wail came from the other room. Nick set his phone on the island and jogged down the hall.

Cassie watched him with worry in her eyes.

Our eyes locked—hers, green mirrors of my own.

Cassie and Nick were a study in opposites attracting. She was bubbly with hidden wisdom. He was serious with hidden playfulness.

But her gaze was dark.

"You feel it too? That's why you couldn't sleep tonight?"

I nodded. If I closed my eyes, I could almost see a pair of amber eyes watching me like I was a mystery they longed to solve.

"I don't know what it is, though, Cass." It was more than the shadowy fingers of dark magic that brushed my senses, a sickly tingle like stepping through a spider's web.

This magic? It wasn't entirely unpleasant. Far from it.

She spooned the tea blend into a tea ball. "I've felt the darkness for days. But there's something else too, something…" She trailed off.

I gazed out the window into the inky black shadows of night.

"Something magical. Something wild," I whispered roughly. "Coming right for Willow Creek."

Coming right for me.

My hand went to my chest, to the rose quartz on its silver chain. The stone burned warm against my skin, like one of those heated stones they used in hot-stone massages. It was usually a cool, calming presence.

Everything was changing.

Well, *something* was changing.

But I knew better than anyone that when something changed, it sometimes took everything else with it.

Aiden
Present Day: Shortly Before Midnight

I tossed a few more logs on the nearest bonfire, one of several burning at the annual gathering of the East Coast shifters. This year, the Shenandoah Shifters had opened their home up to us—a remote corner of Virginia's Shenandoah National Park, one surrounded by a series of protective spells and therefore shielded from prying human eyes.

Well, we *were* human—technically. With just a dash extra.

Sparks flew into the air. The ground was damp from recent rains, so the chance of wildfire was low, but we were still careful.

On the other side of the bonfire, Maddox, a coyote shifter, gave a wild yip, then tossed his head back and laughed at something his companion, a bear shifter, said. Normally, I'd join in the laughter.

But tonight?

I sensed an energy only I seemed to notice. Around me, shifters laughed. A drum circle had formed a ways down, and I heard the drums beating, the low chanting. I could see the female shifters dancing, spinning in circles with arms overhead, fingers stretched toward the sacred moon.

She was waning toward new in the night sky. I propped myself on one elbow and lay against my sleeping bag. The July air was sticky and warm, even at midnight, so I wouldn't need the sleeping bag's warmth, although it had kept out the cold everywhere from Colorado to Maine to Alberta.

I blocked out all sounds until all I heard was the pop of logs, the gentle crackle of the bonfire. It lulled me into a not-quite-sleep. My eyes drifted shut, and I recognized the coming lucid trance to follow.

I stood. I knew the trance needed to happen, but the shifters' nighttime gathering wasn't the place. I gave a nod to Maddox. He quirked an eyebrow but said nothing as I jogged off into the woods.

I didn't go far before I stripped down, my clothes a pile at the base of a pine tree. Shifters didn't care much about seeing each other naked. *You have to strip in order to shift*, as the old shifter joke went.

But the magic that was about to course through me? That the others would feel, and I didn't want to disrupt the party.

My body arched in a pleasant shiver. Some shifters said the change was orgasmic. It wasn't the painful cracking of bone that one might expect.

No. It was an ancient, wild magic that swept through us, like a cool rain washing over drought-stricken earth.

I let the magic take me. Within a matter of seconds, the world looked different.

A sort of smile curved my lips. The earth's magic felt raw, tingling beneath my paws. Though my fur appeared gray to my eyes—I wasn't colorblind in human form, but in fox form, reds and greens looked gray to me—I knew it to be a deep, rusty orange.

I always knew you'd be a fox, my father told me once. He never said why.

A shiver raked me, a memory of sickly magic. Not tonight. I wouldn't think of what my father had demanded of me — not tonight, not in this sacred, mystical place.

I gave a low yip, then another. Then, what the hell, another, for sheer delight. I took off running.

When I reached a clearing, I stared up at the moon.

It was time.

I sat, the heavy, listing energy drawing me down into the earth mother's waiting arms.

I didn't vision-journey often, but tonight? Tonight, I sensed the universe had something to tell me.

A painful howl cut through me. I staggered back in the vision, though my fox form slept on the forest floor.

A man sat in the center of a bed, a tangle of sheets and covers around him. His blond hair was long and in need of a thorough brushing. His beard was full.

But it was his eyes that caught me, that drew me in. They were the kind of baby blues the old clichés spoke about.

But they were haunted.

They met my own, though I wasn't there — not really. Only in spirit form, on the astral plane.

The man reached out to me.

"Evan, it's okay." Another man entered the room.

Oh, Goddess.

I recognized them, though more than a decade had passed since last I'd seen them.

Evan and Nick Felson. My cousins.

Nick entered and sat down on the bed. His mannerisms were paternal in nature, gentle. "It's just another storm rolling through."

"Nick?" A woman's voice this time, softly calling. A blond wisp of a woman peeked in the door, her willowy frame clad in an old-fashioned nightgown. "Is it the storm, you think?"

Nick nodded, his focus on his brother.

This was not the Evan I remembered. Even all those years ago, Evan was...mischievous. He'd been eleven. I'd been twelve.

It was the year I'd learned I was a shifter. The following summer, my father announced my brother and I wouldn't visit our Great-Aunt Ginny anymore. *A bad influence,* my mother said.

It was bullshit, but then, my father preferred money to magic, big bank accounts to big dreams, sailboats to spell books.

But this man, in a sea of torment? It wasn't Evan. Not the Evan I remembered.

"More lepidolite?" the woman asked. "To help him stay calm through the storm?"

Nick raked a hand through his hair. "Maybe?" He tugged at the shaggy strands.

The woman tilted her head. "Maybe more of that tea Vi made?"

Nick nodded slowly. Evan whimpered. "Yeah."

"I'll text her to bring more."

Nick stood up. "No, don't wake her."

"She's already awake. Can't sleep. I feel it."

"She shouldn't be driving in the storm."

"Vi's capable. She can handle it." The woman touched his arm. I saw the tension in Nick's body release. He loved her; that much was clear. "You worry too much. About everyone. Let's focus on Evan tonight. That's where our attention needs to be."

He wrapped his arms around her, running his hands up and down her back. "You're right, Cassie." He kissed the top of her head, then drew away. "Text her. If she's up for it."

The woman—Cassie—stood on tiptoe and kissed his cheek. "Okay."

Thunder rumbled. Evan tilted his head back as though he were in pain. Nick sat down beside him. He reached for his twin brother, but Evan moved out of his reach.

"Why, Goddess?" Nick whispered. "Why would you bring him back to me like this?"

Bring him back? Back from what? The energy in the room made my head pound, my vision blurring.

Here, the shadows dwell.

The words were spoken in a familiar voice—my mentor, Aurora. She was a raven shifter and a witch. She'd mentored me in the magic of both—the shifter's wild magic, the witch's occult wisdom.

What shadows?

They tug on us all. Do what you can. Into the woods you go...

Already in the woods, Aurora.

Her warm laughter washed over me, like slipping into a hot bath on a cold night. *Another wood. A place that is not a place. A spell made manifest...*

Cryptic.

And then I felt her presence slide away, and the shadows of the room where Evan sat tingled around me once more. I moved in closer. Evan watched me.

"You remember me, cousin?" I asked, moving in. Nick didn't seem to notice my presence, but Evan was aware.

Something was off...As a shifter, I sensed people's energies easily—the way it moved through their bodies, where it was blocked.

Evan's?

His energy was burning, exploding.

Even in astral form, I felt the raw pain of it. His senses were overloaded by something. But what? I couldn't tell.

Evan met my eyes. His were blue pools of burning pain. "Make. It. Stop."

Nick grasped his brother's shoulder, but Evan jerked away. "We're working on it. I swear, Ev. I swear."

Though I stood at the foot of the bed, I felt a presence behind me. Like a feather brushing my skin.

Air magic.

"Vi's coming." The woman Nick called Cassie stepped into the room, leaning against a dresser covered with a lace runner and a yellow pitcher and wash basin, a green glass vase of wildflowers beside it.

Her brow furrowed. "Do you feel that?"

Nick came to stand beside her, his hand seeking hers. "Feel what?"

She shook her head. "I don't know. A shift in energy of some kind."

Nick closed his eyes. "I feel...a distant fire. Vi, maybe?"

Cassie shrugged. "Probably." Lightning flashed outside the window, thunder rumbling hot on its heels.

An image flashed through my mind, then, a strange yet familiar magic, a freckled face framed by red hair, surrounded by tendrils of amber fire magic. My lips curled into a smile of pleasure. I didn't know her, yet I did.

"The soul remembers what the mind forgets," Aurora always said.

And then, I tumbled back into my body, out of the astral and into the clearing once more.

The sky above was cloudless. I stretched, arching my spine, trying to bring movement back into my body.

My senses were on high alert, my body itching and restless.

I ran back to my clothes and shoved them on, then booked it back to camp, where my van was parked, waiting. I fished my keys out of my pocket.

"Aiden? Hey, Aiden!" I turned to see Maddox heading in my direction. "What's up with you?"

"I've got to go."

"Go where?" He leaned against the van's exterior, a mural of a mountain range beneath a starry sky. "Everything all right?"

"To Willow Creek, Virginia. It's my cousin."

"Willow Creek?"

He stepped out of the way as I unlocked the door and hopped into the driver's seat. "Hey." He speared me with a wild, brown-eyed gaze. "Be careful. There's something stirring down there. All the Virginia covens are gossiping about it. Trouble brewing in Willow Creek. Their coven vanished."

"No..." Aunt Ginny? Cousin Maeve? Come to think of it, they hadn't appeared in my vision. And if something magical and dark had its claws in Evan, his mom and grandmother would surely be there.

Damn. I had to get to Willow Creek.

"Thanks for the warning." I turned the key in the ignition and clicked my seatbelt into place. The last song I'd been listening to, "Have You Ever Seen the Rain?" by CCR, blared. I turned it down. I rolled down the window.

Maddox studied me. "Watch your six."

I waved, but he was already in the rearview, and my eyes were already fixed on the road ahead.

CHAPTER TWO

Vi

I didn't—couldn't—sleep the rest of the night. With a cup of tea and a few crystals—grounding crystals seemed to work best—Evan had fallen asleep around two. Nick and Cassie had padded off to bed sometime around three. I felt bad. They were running the farm on a few hours a sleep per night, max, while trying to end the curse on Evan and figure out how to rescue the rest of the coven. If they were calling me in the middle of the night, I knew they were beyond exhausted—and scared.

As for me? I didn't have a doubt I'd be watching the sun rise over the Blue Ridge Mountains soon enough. I poured myself another glass of water. My phone's presence tugged at me seductively from my bag, a siren's call of Internet rabbit holes. The web was awash with an endless variety of magical DIYS these days, everything from tarot spreads to crystal combinations.

I took a sip of my water.

Freedom. That's what Cassie called this place—her first taste of freedom. In so many ways, Willow Creek was that for me too. But our childhoods had been different, to say the least. Raised by my great-grandparents and lorded over by her older brother—my grandfather—Cassie had been stifled, watched like a hawk, prohibited even the most basic of freedoms, like a walk in the woods.

By the time I was around, Great-Grandma was in a nursing home, succumbing to dementia, a shadow of herself. And Cassie's father, my great-grandfather, passed before my mother was even born.

And Granddad? He'd been haunted. Haunted by his past. Haunted, I learned soon enough, by who he was. He'd raised me after my mom passed. I never knew my dad.

Granddad had done the best he could. He'd loved me, and I knew now he'd shown me kindness he'd never shown his rebellious little sister.

He'd also been a witch, one taught to fear magic—to fear himself. And so, he'd sought escape in the easiest way he could find—at the bottom of a whiskey bottle.

When he'd died in that crash—when I was thirteen—I'd felt his soul release. I wasn't there when it happened, but I woke up from my sleep, saw a shadow of a figure in the corner of my room.

"Going away now, girlie. Get some rest." His voice was rough, not with drink but with sadness.

I felt a brush of fingers against my hair. "Don't know where you got that red hair from. Must've been your daddy. Your mama was blond. Like me and your aunt Cassie. I should've done you better, sweet Vivienne. But She says..." His voice broke. "She says the soul must journey on now. Lessons in the shadows..."

With a shiver of cold air, he'd vanished.

When I'd heard the sirens, I knew.

Running in bare feet, down that gravel road. Someone—an EMT, maybe—catching me, keeping me away.

Sometimes at night, when I couldn't sleep, I almost thought I'd turn a corner and he'd be there, his eyes sad, his mouth turned down in a sorrowful frown.

"Vi?" A gentle voice pried me out of my waking dream. I turned, sloshing water out of my glass. Cassie stood there, her hair tousled from sleep.

I didn't say anything. Didn't have to. She wrapped her arms around me. I was ten inches taller than my great-aunt, but Cassie's presence was as big as her heart. And, thanks to a magical mishap that trapped her spirit in a tree for nearly five decades, I was somehow a year older than she was.

"Thinking of him?"

"I don't know why." I sniffed. "I'll go so long, you know?"

"You finally met his sister. That had to dredge up some memories."

"It's not that. It's the magic. How can you sleep? It's so..." I turned away, setting my water glass on the counter and pacing along the hardwood floor between the counter and the island. "Like every nerve ending is on edge."

Cassie watched me. I felt her gaze, the assessment in it. "Is it the shadows, you think? The rising darkness?"

I shook my head. "It's. Goddess, Aunt Cass. I don't know what."

She smirked. "Finally calling me auntie?"

I laughed, the sound rough. "Can't do it in public. People already think we're weird."

"Not weird." Cassie crossed the room to a cookie jar in the shape of a basket of green apples. She set it on the island and handed me a gingersnap. She bit into one, crumbs trailing down her chin. "We're eccentric. In the best possible way."

I took a cookie, then another.

"Do you ever eat vegetables?" Cassie asked.

I feigned offense. "Of course! I just prefer sweets."

She pulled a glass jug of milk out of the fridge and poured two small glasses.

A swath of lights and a crunch of gravel halted the conversation. I peered out the kitchen window into the darkness. A large van came to a stop at the end of the driveway, beside Nick's pickup and my Subaru.

"Who is that?" Cassie said.

I shrugged. "Not Bailee. All she's got is that little yellow Bug of hers."

"Probably someone who got lost. All these folks relying on that GDS stuff."

"GPS," I corrected.

"I'll get Nick, just to be safe." She slipped away down the hall.

I stared out the window. There was a firm shutting of a car door, and then a tall figure strode toward the house. I moved toward the back door, unsure what to expect, but wanting to tell off whoever was strolling up to the house in the middle of the night.

An energy washed over me.

No. Not washed. It hit me like a rogue wave.

My legs felt weak now, made of gelatin, but all I could do was stare at the man on the other side of the screen door. Amber eyes peered at me, through me, into the depths. I felt energy centers in my body awaken, pools of energy quivering.

"Hello?" he said, his voice a deep, fine Southern rumble. He peered in, out of the darkness of the back porch. "Is Nick here?"

I just stared at him, dumbstruck.

He studied me, cocking his head. "Didn't mean to wake you, but it didn't seem like the sort of thing that could wait until a decent hour. Is Nick around, by chance?"

"What. Is. Going. On?" Nick stomped into the kitchen, shirtless and grumpy.

I pointed at the window with my thumb. "Some guy asking for you." The words sounded froggy, and I swallowed, my throat dry.

Nick muttered something unintelligible and squinted into the darkness. "Can I help—" He paused, staring at the mystery man. "Aiden?"

"Hey, cousin. Long time."

"Yeah…What are you doing here?'

"You know, had a vision at a shifters' gathering in Shenandoah, seemed like y'all could use some help, so, since I was in the neighborhood…"

"That's…" To say Nick sounded confused would've been an understatement. "I don't even know. Get in here."

He swung open the screen door.

Aiden was so tall that his dark hair nearly brushed the top of the doorframe. His build was athletic, but lean, and an image of him running through an emerald green forest under a silver moon flickered through my imagination.

He smiled at me. "Aiden McPherson. Sorry about startling you."

"I…" My mind blanked. "Hi."

His smile turned into this soft sort of smile—kind of dopey but sexy at the same time, with a little hidden mischief twinkling in those molten amber eyes—and all I knew was that I was staring up at him like some lovestruck middle-schooler fangirling over a celebrity crush. Despite his navy-blue "born to run" t-shirt and tattered jeans, he reminded me of a professor in the making, the sort of man who'd teach anthropology in casual attire while his female students swooned.

He offered his hand. I shook off the brain fog and took his hand. His fingers were long and slender, his palms broad and square shaped. The fire magic I kept tucked away crackled in my veins as we briefly shook hands.

Afterward, he turned away, rubbing his palms together, and faced Nick.

But the fire inside of me didn't retreat.

Nick raked a hand through his hair. "Sorry. We've been through a lot lately. Did you say...shifter?"

Aiden nodded, his gaze flickering back to me for a second. Curiosity. I didn't know why. He'd said he was a shifter. Hadn't he met a witch with fire magic before?

He turned away from me. "Yeah. My powers showed up the full moon after my thirteenth birthday. Because adolescence isn't already enough of a bitch."

"Is that why you never came back?" Nick raised an eyebrow. "I think you know that we, more than anyone, would've understood."

"You know my parents. Money before magic and that whole spiel. But I'm here now." He furrowed his brow. His voice seemed to catch on the word *now*. "Where's Evan?"

Nick swallowed, his face paling. Cassie stepped forward.

"Evan's not well," she said simply, all full of gentle manners where I couldn't find two words to string together.

Aiden nodded. "I know. That's why I'm here." He cocked his head. "Who are you?"

Cassie smiled one of those light-up-a-room smiles. "Cassie Gearhart. Nick's, uh..." She eyed Nick, as if suddenly unsure how to introduce herself.

"This is my girlfriend, Cassie. This is Vi. She's Cassie's uh..."

I stepped forward. "I'm a distant relation." Best keep the explanation simple. We didn't know why Aiden was here, after all.

Aiden quirked an eyebrow. "Well, that wasn't a weird series of introductions at all."

The silence that descended wasn't comfortable and amiable. It was awkward, filled with unspoken truths and questions no one dared give voice to.

Aiden cleared his throat. "Can I...Can I see Evan? Like I said, that's sort of why I'm here."

Aiden

Ye gods.

Nick and his girlfriend and her, uh, distant relation, were staring at me like I was a first-rate weirdo.

To be fair, I'd sort of barged in on their lives in the middle of the night, dropped the whole "I'm a shifter" news like Zeus hurling a random lightning bolt, and requested an audience with my cousin.

Nick cracked his knuckles and turned toward the window, though the sky was still dark. "It's not that simple."

Well, I'd stepped in it. "Nick." I kept my voice low. "This isn't a social call. I had a vision. I know."

He turned toward me, his blue gaze piercing. I matched it with my own. Nick had always been intense, but there was a fierce strength in him now I didn't remember.

He'd embraced his magic. That was what had changed. The fox in me bowed his head, acknowledging Nick's power. I was on his turf. This was his coven—the bubbly waif in a vintage nightgown, and the fire witch whose mere touch had sent waves of pleasant heat shooting through me.

Nick studied me, his brow furrowed. "A vision? Of Evan?"

I nodded. The weight of their stares was about a thousand tons. I shook my shoulders loose and pressed on. "I've spent the last couple years working on my magical skills. No one in my family could tell me what it meant to be a shifter, how the magic worked. So, I set off on my own to learn." I tried not to think of that moment two years ago that was the catalyst for my journey.

Nick crossed his arms over his chest. "A little bit of magical study and you're going to waltz in the door and heal Evan when the rest of us couldn't?"

I shifted my sight ever so slightly, letting the fox see what my human eyes couldn't. My mentor, Aurora, had taught me to let my fox take over without a full shift. My magic wasn't as strong in my human form, but I could see a little—enough to see that Nick's heart chakra was blocked. He was grieving.

I asked the fox to sleep and released the magic. "It's not like that," I started to explain.

Nick ran his hands through already tousled hair, a growl of seeming frustration rising from his throat.

Cassie stepped between us and touched his shoulder. "Why don't we sleep on it? We could all use the rest."

"I think it might work," Vi said. Her voice was soft, a little husky. My fox stirred, leaning in. "He might have a perspective that we don't," she continued. "Shifter magic is different from witch magic."

We all turned to face her, and she shifted her stance, her hand flying to the pale pink gemstone at her throat.

"Could you two stop staring at her like that? It's kind of distressing," Cassie said. It sounded like a gentle suggestion, but it was a command. She didn't look older than any of the rest of us, yet her energy *was* older somehow. She turned to the other witch, who was gazing right back at me, as if she, too, sensed the strange energy swirling between us. "Vi, I think you might be on to something."

Vi cleared her throat. She grabbed a cookie from a cookie jar, the scent of ginger and home-baked goodness hitting my nostrils. She took a bite, chewing thoughtfully before continuing. "It's been a week, and we're no closer to finding out what's causing Evan's condition." She took another bite and swallowed. "I'm just saying, if Aiden had a vision, and that vision was sent to him by the Goddess, there must be a reason."

I held my breath, waiting for the others to react. Vi polished off her cookie and brushed crumbs off her top — a black crop top with a purple rose emblazoned on it. "Rose amongst the thorns," it read. She wore a pair of high-waisted black yoga pants, her red hair tied back in a loose ponytail, stray strands framing her face. She had a smattering of freckles across her nose and cheekbones. Faerie kisses, Aunt Ginny used to call such freckles.

Cassie turned to Nick, clasping his hand. "Well, what do you think?"

Nick's lips were set in a firm line, betraying nothing but displeasure. With my unexpected visit? It was, as

Mom would say, the worst form — showing up uninvited. And emptyhanded, too. Except for a soul full of magic — and Mom would remind me that didn't count.

Except here. In Willow Creek. At Aunt Ginny's house. The one place showing up with nothing but magic actually meant something.

Nick glared at me. "Weren't you in law school?"

I laughed, a dark, bitter sort of sound. I shrugged. "I quit. Long story." I probably could've been a good lawyer. But I didn't really want to be in the courtroom. Truth be told, I'd always preferred reading in the park with a stack of books from the library. It hadn't even mattered what the subject was.

"Okay…" Nick sighed. He threw up his hands. "We'll try it. Just a brief session. In the morning. It's been a long night. Evan is finally asleep." He cast a don't-cross-me glare at all of us. "He needs to rest, and Vi's tea is helping. Let's keep it that way. Got it?"

We all nodded. I was itching to get to it — and honestly, I preferred the hours between twilight's descent and dawn's early light. My inner fox craved the moonlight, the starlight, the shadowed forest. But Nick made a fair point. No need to disturb Evan now.

Cassie whispered something to Nick, and he nodded in my direction. "You can take the couch. Vi, you want Gran's room?" he said.

"Sure."

He clapped me on the back. "Welcome back." Then he headed back to bed.

Cassie turned to me. "You're hungry. Want me to fix you something before I try to get some sleep?"

"No. I can manage." My stomach rumbled at the suggestion, though, betraying me.

She grinned. "I insist."

"Whatever's easiest. Don't go to any trouble."

"Sit."

I pulled out a chair to the kitchen table — the same one from all those years ago. Some things in the house had changed, but for the most part, the Saunders Family Farm remained the same.

Cassie pulled out sandwich fixings. "Cup of tea?"

"That would be amazing." At law school, there was maybe one other person in my cohort who drank hot tea, but she'd been older than me by a few years. All the guys thought I was crazy, drinking hot tea all the time.

Vi studied me. "Something grounding? Calming? Soothing? You name it, I've got it."

"Hmm. Show me what you've got." I grinned. "I'm something of an aficionado."

Vi laughed, the sound low, throaty. I got the sense she had a secret sense of humor, one she kept hidden from the world. "A man after my own heart."

She pulled out a few mason jars, each labeled in calligraphic script. "Green tea and citrus zest. Energizing," one read. "Fire Magic Blend," said another. I picked that one up, unscrewed the cap, and inhaled. Cinnamon. A bit of orange zest, perhaps? A few other ingredients.

"This one. Definitely."

She smiled, seeming pleased. "That one's my favorite."

"Do you sell them?"

"Just at the farmers' market and the local co-op. I want to open a shop, but I'm still saving up for it."

Before I could ask for more details, Cassie slid a plate in front of me. The next thing I knew, I was wolfing down a turkey, cheese, and avocado sandwich with fresh tomato slices and romaine lettuce.

"Wow. You were hungry," Cassie said. "Do you want something else?"

I brushed crumbs out of my beard. "Sorry about my lack of table manners. I drove straight here." And I usually snacked after a shift, since I burned so many calories in the process. I rose and grabbed the canister of cookies from the island, then returned, holding it out to Cassie and Vi. They each took a cookie, and I polished off two in about five seconds.

"I have to ask before I do any energy work with Evan. What happened to the coven?"

The color drained from Cassie's face. Vi shook her head.

"They're trapped," Cassie whispered, as though it pained her. "On a magical plane. By Nick's father."

"Nick's father? He didn't have magic."

"It turns out, he did. And he's trying to use it to steal all of the magic of Willow Creek and harness it for himself."

I couldn't help the curse that passed my lips, though I'd tried to limit my foul language since I started doing energy work. I didn't want to put negative energy into the world—not any more than was already out there.

The kettle started to whistle, and Vi jumped up and removed it before it could wake Nick and Evan.

I closed my eyes.

This was so much worse than I'd thought.

CHAPTER THREE

Vi

Two cups of tea later, I convinced a constantly yawning Cassie to go to bed. She squeezed my shoulders before she made her way down the hall.

I refilled Aiden's mug, then my own.

The expression on his face was grim. In the past week, I'd met more magical folks then I had previously known in my entire life.

But then, once I'd entered foster care, I'd been too focused on keeping my magic secret. And before that magic was a curse word as far as my grandfather was concerned. We did *not* talk about magic when I was growing up.

I'd had to read books about a certain boy wizard in the school library in the fifth grade—because even fictional witchcraft was forbidden in our household. Period. End of discussion.

Aiden leaned back and sipped his tea. "I'm curious," he said, his voice a low rumble. "How do you fit into all of this?"

I studied the scene outside the window of the farmhouse kitchen. The slightest lightening of the sky — the most magical shade of blue I'd ever seen — hinted at the coming sunrise. Where did I even begin? "Well, Cassie's my great-aunt."

"How does that happen? I mean, I sense magic afoot — obviously."

I couldn't help but smile at his wry humor — and admire his nonchalance at my revelation. "The Guardian of the Crossroads of Magic turned her into a tree. Somehow, that magic allowed her to Rip Van Winkle her way from the 1970s to the twenty-first century."

"That's…" He exhaled, his brow furrowing in a look of deep thought. I sensed Aiden was a man prone to deep thoughts and constant mulling of things, and I liked that. "I've never heard of anything like that. I knew the Guardian was powerful, but it's almost like…"

"Like she found a workaround to time travel?"

"Basically. Kind of fascinating."

I nodded. I traced the handle of my mug with my thumb. "I've learned more about magic since coming to Willow Creek than I ever imagined possible."

"Where are you from?"

"Georgia."

"Me too. I grew up just outside Savannah. My dad owns a law firm there. My family's estate isn't far from the city."

Law firm? Estate? "Sounds fancy." I fingered the rose quartz on my neck. "And you live in a van now?" The words escaped before I could censor them. I winced. I was usually so careful with how I chose my words. Must've been lack of sleep.

I opened my mouth to apologize for my gaffe, but he chuckled, the sound warm, washing over me like spring sunshine after a long winter. His eyes darkened, though, their amber deepening like glowing embers. "I needed a fresh start, and that meant leaving behind the life my parents built for me. I'm okay with it, though. Money..." He swirled the contents of his mug, then shrugged. "It's not this silver bullet that solves all of your problems."

"I know." My voice was low. I studied that perfect blue of the not-quite-dawn, remembering. "When I was little, I used to think if we'd had more money, Granddad would've quit drinking, that things would've been better. But that...that was never going to happen. Because he was running away, and no amount of money would've helped him run far enough."

Those amber eyes studied me. They were intense, hinting at an analytical mind, but far, far from unkind. "What was he running from?"

I managed a weak smile. "From who he was. A witch. Someone with fire magic singing in his veins."

He nodded. "He's not the only one. My parents, the whole family, we've got magic in our blood thing. We don't speak about it. My brother went to school, got his business degree, takes this potion that suppresses his ability—or need—to shift. My dad does the same thing."

"Where did your magic come from?"

"My grandfather was Aunt Ginny's brother. He left Willow Creek and went to college in North Carolina, then married a woman whose family had money in Savannah. Set up a law firm there, one that my dad inherited. My grandfather was a shifter. He died young, before the potion to suppress the shift was perfected. It took a toll on his body, Dad said."

A silence passed over us, not exactly comfortable, but not exactly awkward either. It was the sort of silence that reverberated with unspoken truths, as though it were full of static and spells. There we were, two magical souls from magical families who'd tried to make a legacy of hiding their true selves.

And here we were now, sitting in the kitchen of a farmhouse where magic was welcomed, embraced, celebrated.

I smiled. "This house is like a lighthouse, isn't it? A sort of magical beacon, calling all the lost magical souls home."

Aiden nodded. "I never thought of it in that exact way, but yeah. That's the perfect description."

I picked up the empty teapot and our now-empty mugs and carried them to the kitchen sink, rinsing them out and listening to the earliest of birds serenade the sun.

When I turned away, Aiden stood at the picture window behind the kitchen table, muscled arms folded over his chest. I caught a tattoo on one arm—an orangish red fox, with vivid amber eyes in almost metallic ink, sitting majestically in front of green and blue mountains, a moon rising above.

"Your ink is gorgeous."

He glanced down at his left arm, almost absently. "Thanks. An artist friend in Santa Fe did it."

"Wow. So, you've been all over."

"Pretty much."

"What's your favorite place you've been?"

He stroked his chin stubble, as if considering. But then he smiled like he'd known the answer all along. "Here. There's a nexus of magic in this town, in these mountains. It…" He shrugged, as if he couldn't put that magic into words.

I studied the dimly lit mountains, still cloaked in the last remaining vestiges of night. I knew what he meant. "It sings," I whispered.

He nodded. "It really does."

Not entirely of my own volition, my fingers reached out toward the tattoo. I curled them and tucked my hand against my side, a strange, deep ache rising inside of me.

"Art is a form of magic," he continued, gazing down at me. "And when the ink has magic in it, well, so much the better." His voice was rough, a husky, thoughtful murmur. That ache grew worse inside of me.

I turned so he could examine my own tattoo—a teacup on my right arm, tendrils of steam rising up to mingle with the crescent moon and stars above. Vines danced around it, covered in thorns and tiny purple flowers.

His long fingers hovered over my skin, and a mini sigh escaped my lips. I felt the energy of his careful gaze slide down my skin, examining the artist's careful design and execution.

"Was your artist a witch?" he asked.

I nodded. "A friend in Savannah, a member of my first coven." After graduating high school and aging out of the foster care system, I'd made my way to Savannah, still working up the courage to come to Willow Creek. I'd found Aunt Cassie's picture and a slip of paper with the name of a farm—this farm, to be precise—in Willow Creek written on it when I was thirteen. I'd waited eight years before I came here.

Just in time to meet Aunt Cassie.

"She had a gift," Aiden continued. "With ink and with magic. Your tattoo is the perfect combination of both."

I smiled. "I think so." I'd met a few people who made ridiculous assumptions about people with tattoos—that I was a bad girl, that I liked to party, that I was irresponsible. But Aiden, he *got* it. It wasn't about communicating anything to anyone else. It was about celebrating who I was—as a witch, as an individual, as a woman.

He shoved his hands into his pockets. He cleared his throat as though trying to break some strange spell that had woven around us. "We should try to get a couple hours of sleep. I have a feeling tomorrow is going to be a long day."

"You're right. I think Cassie set some blankets on the sofa for you."

"Yeah." He turned away and began to pad off into the living room. "Vi?"

"Yes?" The word came out soft, almost a croak.

"Good night."

A smile flickered across my lips, butterflies dancing in my stomach. It wasn't like me, to open my energy so easily to someone I didn't know. It felt easy, pleasant even, like twilight breeze tugging at my hair after a long, hot day.

I made my way to Ginny's old room, which Cassie kept ready in case Bailee or I wanted to stay the night.

Fire magic sang a warm, sensuous lullaby under my skin as I listened to the rain beat against the window.

Aiden

I woke up to the sound of someone clearing their throat. I cracked my eyes open to see Nick staring down at me, his lips quirking in a not-quite-repressed smile.

"Wow," Nick said. "You really are a fox shifter. Morning, woodland creature."

I blinked. His words had a sharp clarity to their timbre that felt off. The room didn't look quite right.

I squirmed on the sofa.

Crap.

I'd shifted into my fox form. In the middle of the night, like some gods-damn adolescent experiencing nocturnal transformations.

Must've been those dreams last night. Wild, hot dreams laced with fire and magic and kisses stolen underneath the stars.

Dreams that felt far too real.

I stared up at Nick, unable to defend myself, embarrassed as hell. This hadn't happened in, well, years. I was twenty-four years old—well past this awkward stage of life.

I jumped off the sofa and stretched, then gave Nick an annoyed yip before I sauntered down the hall and into the bathroom, where I shifted back into my now-naked human form in a tingle of magical energy.

I grabbed a towel and wrapped it around my waist before creeping back into the living room.

Cassie walked in from the kitchen, an innocent smile on her face suggesting that she'd seen the fox curled up on the sofa but was far too polite to say so. "Morning. How do you take your eggs?"

Nick chuckled. "Stolen from the henhouse?"

I shot him a glare, catching Cassie's playful smirk out of the corner of my eye. "I'm not picky," I said with a shrug.

My clothes were gone, a victim of the magic that accompanied my shift. Many a shifter had lost perfectly good clothing or a precious piece of jewelry during an unplanned shift.

"Do you usually sleep in your, uh, animal form?" Nick asked, taking a sip of coffee from what looked like a handmade coffee mug—a deep navy color with a crescent moon over a backdrop of mountains.

I fidgeted. "Have you always been this cheeky? I thought Evan was the mischievous one."

Nick's eyes filled with solemn shadows.

"Shit. I'm sorry," I said, the words tumbling out. "I wasn't thinking."

"I don't..." Nick cleared his throat, but all traces of amusement were gone. "I don't know if he'll ever be the same."

"I'm going to do everything I can. Two years, okay? Two years, I've done nothing but travel and study. I've studied magic in more varieties than I can count. Philosophies of magic from all over the world. Reiki. Shifter magic. Elemental magic. Faerie lore. If any of that can help, I swear to you, I'll make it happen."

Nick nodded. He was once more the serious one—all work, no play, Nick Felson.

The image of Evan, twelve years old, the Peter Pan of our little band of Lost Boys, flashed through my mind.

That Evan, the one we all knew and loved, couldn't be gone.

"I'm sorry I waited so long."

"I should've reached out," Nick said.

Silence crept in. The sound of Cassie taking a cast iron frying pan out of a drawer broke the shared melancholy. I suspected it was hard to be melancholy around Cassie for too long. "There are blueberry muffins on the table, coffee in the coffee press, and scrambled eggs, bacon, and potatoes are on the way," she said.

"I'll be back in a few minutes. Need to feed the chickens and check on a few things," Nick said, dropping a kiss on Cassie's cheek. She smiled up at him, this warm adoration in her eyes. He glanced at me. "Make sure a certain fox hasn't visited the henhouse."

I rolled my eyes. He shoved on a pair of gray sneakers and strode out the door.

"I might grab some clothes from the van and hop in the shower, unless you need some help with breakfast," I said, watching Nick cross the yard in wide strides. There wasn't much time to be wasted where Evan was concerned.

And beautiful fire witches, steamy dreams, and surprise sleep-shifting aside, Evan was the reason I was here.

"No. I don't mind. I kind of like having people to cook for. Gives me something to keep myself occupied. You could check in on Evan, though—make sure he's still asleep."

"Sure."

In the van, I tugged on an olive-green shirt and a pair of dark khaki cargo pants.

The van once belonged to a traveling bluegrass guitarist. I'd found it advertised online and figured it was the perfect vehicle for traveling the country. I wasn't sure where I was going when I paid the guy eight hundred bucks for it and rebuilt the engine—only that it would get me where I needed to go.

The outside of the van was painted cobalt blue with a smattering of stars. Emerald green mountains made up the lower half of the scene, with woodland creatures frolicking near a stream tumbling over rocks.

Willow Creek. That's what the scene reminded me of. The mountains in the background. The creek itself. The magic and the wildness.

It meant something. I just didn't know what yet.

I slipped back into the house.

Music played low, a bit of folk music to serenade the Sunday sun. Cassie scrambled eggs in a stainless-steel mixing bowl and poured them into a waiting skillet as I passed through the kitchen.

I pushed the door to Maeve's old room open—the same room I'd visited in last night's vision. The hinges didn't even squeak.

Evan lay on his side, his body curled tightly into itself, shifting restlessly in a tangle of covers.

A wave of energy hit me. Not the gentle sort of wave that teases you like a summer breeze. Not the molten heat with which Vi's fire magic met me the night before.

My lips formed a silent scream. I clenched my teeth together to lock it away.

The next wave knocked me to my knees.

I grabbed the nearby dresser, painted an aged turquoise. The water pitcher and basin atop rattled as my full weight shook the dresser.

I blinked.

Evan sat there, watching me.

But he wasn't the old Evan. His hair—even in middle school, he'd always glanced in a mirror before heading out the door—was unkempt. His beard—I couldn't picture Evan with a beard or even a five o'clock shadow—was long, as though he hadn't shaved in a year.

But it was his eyes. They locked with mine.

I managed to sit on the edge of the bed, to take his hand. Mine shook from the sheer force of dark energy swirling in the room—like trying to go for a stroll in gale-force winds. His fingers were long, the nails broken, some split clear down the center.

"Evan, what happened?"

He opened his mouth to speak, but no words came out. The vision hit me like a punch in the gut. I doubled over, a vision of a long-forgotten face now burned into my retinas.

Weylin. Evan and Nick's father, a man I scarcely remembered. He'd left when Nick and Evan were in elementary school. No one talked about him much after that.

So, he was a bastard through and through? I'd sort of figured. But how could no one have known that he had magic? Not even Aunt Ginny, the strongest, most capable witch I knew? That seemed impossible. Those of us with magic in our veins could sense another's magic. We felt it like we felt the humidity in the air, the heat of a fire's flames, the brush of a feather, or the plop of a raindrop against the skin.

My stomach churned. Magic was inherently good. It was a force of love, of creativity, of healing, of nature. It was our connection to the natural world and to spirit itself.

Whatever was happening to Evan was a corruption of that goodness.

I held out my free hand.

"Can I check your energy, Evan?"

He frowned at me.

"Do you remember me? It's me, Aiden. Your crazy cousin. We used to skip stones in the swimming hole, remember? You were always mad because I could skip stones farther."

His lips remained in a wordless scowl, but his gaze traveled to my hand, hovering over his chest. I'd opened myself up to reiki energy, ready if need be, but I didn't push.

He nodded.

I started with his crown chakra, then worked my way down through all seven chakras. I didn't push, just a quick scan.

I closed my eyes, the energy pulsing in a great throbbing, like bass loud enough to shatter your eardrums.

There were no obvious signs of physical trauma. If he'd been tortured, it hadn't been physical—and thank the Goddess for that.

I'd managed to block out the worst of the nauseating dark magic, but the longer I stayed this close, the more my teeth ached from clenching my jaw, the more my stomach churned.

If Evan were anyone else, I would've sent him some extra reiki energy for healing.

But this briefest glimpse showed me that wasn't what he needed.

There was something wrong, something I couldn't even begin to understand. It was like Evan's chakras weren't merely blocked. It was like part of him was far away, and every cell in his body was yearning to get back to that lost self.

The pain of it…

I opened my eyes and drew away, my body trembling.

Evan's gaze was fixed on a figure in the doorway.

I stood and turned. Vi stood there, her hair in a loose braid, her fingers clasping the rose quartz stone around her neck.

She watched me, her gaze curious, but the set of her jaw defensive—no, scratch that. Protective. "What are you doing? Does Nick know you're in here?"

I held up my hands in an I-surrender gesture. "It's okay. Cassie asked me to check on him. And I wasn't doing anything. Just a quick scan of his chakras—not manipulating his energy fields in any way."

The tension that had seized her body dissipated, however slightly. "If Cassie said…" She nodded. "Okay. I guess it's okay then."

Cassie peeked into the room. "Bacon and eggs for breakfast, Evan. Can I fix you a plate?"

He turned away, not answering.

Vi and I stepped into the hallway. I shut the door softly behind me. "Has he said anything since he's been back?"

She shook her head. "Not a single word. Did you sense anything just now?"

We rounded the corner into the kitchen. Cassie set a plate of crispy bacon on the table, arranging it amid a bowl of scrambled eggs and a casserole dish of home fries with peppers and onions.

Nick kicked off his shoes, shutting the back door behind him.

We all stopped what we were doing to stare at him. How was he going to react to what I had to tell him?

"What? Do I have chicken droppings in my hair?"

"No." Cassie stood on tiptoe to kiss his cheek. "You're fine. But I have the feeling Aiden has something to tell you."

That warranted an eyebrow raise. "I do?" I mean, I did, but how did she know I'd found something?

"Mm-hmm," she said, nodding.

"Don't ask," Vi said, pouring herself a glass of orange juice and taking a sip. "She just knows things."

"Didn't used to," Cassie said. "Must be the whole time-travel thing."

Nick crossed his arms over his chest and leaned against the doorframe. "Well?" His raised eyebrow dared me to impress him.

I smirked. Had to love how my cousin talked like he was twenty years my senior instead of a year younger. Not that it mattered much these days. I suspected we'd all need Nick's quiet style of leadership when all hell broke loose.

Which, judging by the magic I'd just felt, would be any day now. I swallowed.

"I did a brief scan of Evan's energy centers. I don't know what's causing it, but I can confirm there's no physical injury. He wasn't tortured."

"That's a relief," Cassie said. She frowned. "What about his nails, though?"

"I can't explain that. I don't think it was done to him, though. Maybe it's..." I couldn't bring myself to finish that sentence. It made me sick just to think it.

"Something he was made to do to himself?" Vi whispered.

I could only nod.

"Gods dammit," Nick said. He turned away, staring at the screen door with arms folded.

"There's more."

Nick slowly turned around. All eyes were on me now. I licked my suddenly dry lips. "Nick, there's something missing. Like...like when Evan returned, he left a part of himself behind."

Nick narrowed his gaze. "I don't know what that means."

"Me either," Cassie said. Her voice was low, taut with worry.

I exhaled. "I can't explain it. My fox, my inner shifter, he can sense things I can't. What my fox saw...that's only part of Evan in there. But something is missing. He's not whole. I'm not speaking in metaphors here."

"That doesn't make any sense," Vi said. "Why would someone do that?"

"That's the worst part. I don't know. I don't even know *how* someone would do that, let alone why."

Thunder cracked overhead, shaking the farmhouse. Beside me, Vi jumped, bumping against a chair.

I grabbed the chair before it could topple over.

Her freckled skin blushed ever so slightly as our gazes locked. Her lips fluttered up in a nervous smile. "We've had so many storms this summer."

But something else was troubling her. I could sense Vi's strength, and she wasn't afraid of a clap of thunder. No. But now, in front of Cassie and Nick, wasn't the time to ask. With everything going on with Evan, it was possible Vi had found a piece of the puzzle that Nick and Cassie had overlooked.

"It's the shadows," Cassie said. "There's a dark magic waking up in Willow Creek. I heard the Guardian's screams last night. Maybe Evan hears them too."

Rain thrummed against the metal roof. It used to soothe me, the summer rainstorms when I stayed here as a child. But this storm wasn't a part of nature—not exactly.

This storm? It was nature's way of fighting back with all she had in her arsenal.

Nick and Cassie slipped away to check on Evan.

Vi offered me a glass of juice. I chugged it down, my throat dry, then refilled the glass with water from the tap.

"Aiden?" Her voice was soft and worried.

"Yeah?"

"If the Guardian dies…"

"She's immortal," I pointed out. I remembered that vividly from Aunt Ginny's campfire tales.

"Not invincible."

Was she? Damn, but I didn't know. There was so much I didn't know that it set my teeth on edge. "True."

She plopped down in one of the high-backed chairs that matched the oak table. "If she dies, what happens to the magic she guards?"

I sat at the chair closest to hers, my gaze falling to her hands, fingers twisted together in her lap. Another tattoo, a small triangle, the Pagan symbol for fire, graced her wrist. The scent of amber and patchouli with a hint of vanilla wafted up from her skin. My fox sighed with pleasure. Usually, perfumes overwhelmed my heightened sense of smell, but Vi's perfume seemed made from natural ingredients and thoroughly pleasant.

I focused on Vi's question. It was a troubling one. "I don't know. I'm not sure anyone could say for certain. But..." A blinding flash of lightning lit the sky, the thunder that followed seeming to last forever.

Vi smiled weakly. Those green eyes met with mine. There was fierce honesty in their depths—and a wisdom I somehow suspected others often overlooked. "Then all of that magic she protects would be up for grabs?"

I nodded. "I think that's a possibility." And I doubted it would be a coven of witches who walked firmly in the light who'd seize upon that magic.

She tilted her head back against the chair, sighing. When she tilted her head back down, her eyes practically glowed, like green orbs on a stormy day.

"We can fix it," she said. It sounded like a solemn oath, a fierce vow.

"One thing at a time. Let's help Evan first."

I reached for her hand, squeezing it. She squeezed mine back. The contact was brief, simple. It felt natural, like we were old friends.

Though the dreams I had last night? Hardly about mere friendship. I swallowed, my throat dry again.

She speared me with that quiet warrior gaze again. "Aiden, don't you see? Evan, the Guardian, Cassie. Your magic, mine. It's all connected."

"Tug on one string, tug on them all?"

"Exactly." Her eyes fastened on mine. Something inside of me tightened. I turned away, toward a wall covered in sunflower wallpaper.

A lump formed in my throat. "I was afraid of that."

That way she looked at me, like she had faith in me, in my magic?

Goddess, after two years of study, I thought I'd be ready.

But I wasn't.

CHAPTER FOUR

Vi

The magic in my veins simply sang. It felt like a tingling along the nerve endings, a wild yet pleasant hum of electricity.

I wasn't sure what that meant. I wanted to say it was all the magical happenings of the past few days. I wanted to say it was that Aiden's fox-shifter energy was new and exciting. I wanted to say it was my newfound coven.

But the ache in a down-low place suggested that my womanly side found Aiden every bit as appealing as the witch.

And I didn't...Well, let's just say I'd had only a few boyfriends, and it never went well. Even without my magic, I had built far too many walls to protect far too many secrets. Only a handful of people—my friend Bailee, here in Willow Creek; and Cassie; and another witchy friend, Ivy, back in Savannah—had been able to make it through my defenses.

Granddad hadn't been reliable, but he'd been all I had. After he died, letting people in, even my foster mother, was hard. She'd been kind, fair, a warm person who'd raised her own children and felt called to help kids like me.

I still loved her, still spoke to her every few weeks, but I had so many secrets she'd never know. And secrets? Well, secrets were walls.

I turned toward the window, rubbing my rose quartz pendant between my fingers and watching fat drops of rain fling themselves against the wide expanse of glass. Beyond, low mist clung stubbornly to the blue-green mountains in the distance.

I dropped the crystal, letting it settle against my chest. I needed to break that habit, I reminded myself. Instead, I rubbed my thumb over the opposite wrist, where my tattoo tingled with the memory of Aiden's gaze.

"Did I say something?" Aiden asked.

His lips had curved into a frown. He was the kind of guy you expected to take up beekeeping so he could keep careful notes on their behavior patterns, his words quiet and carefully chosen, with a bit of ready wit waiting underneath. With his hair as black as midnight, his skin slightly tanned from time in the sun, his eyes like amber embers, he seemed equal parts mystic and scholar.

I blinked, realizing that tears were welling up in my eyes.

"It's been a lot lately," I confessed, then promptly bit my lip.

He nodded. "Tell me about it. Last night I'm at the biggest shifter shindig on the East Coast, and now I'm solving mystical riddles in Willow Creek." He poured a cup of tea and handed it to me. The scent of my morning blend—peppermint, lemongrass, spearmint—hit my nostrils.

I couldn't help but smile. He poured himself a cup, leaned against the table, stretching his long legs out in front of him and crossing them at the ankles.

"What brought you here?" he asked.

I swallowed a sip of tea. "An old photograph and a piece of paper."

"Mysterious." He said nothing else, just sipped and watched the rain fall, as if waiting for me to speak.

"When I was thirteen, my grandfather—Cassie's brother—died in a car accident. My mom died when I was a baby; my dad was never around. So, Granddad raised me. After he died, I ended up in foster care. Before the social worker took me to my foster mom's, she let me gather up a few things. I took this old cigar box Granddad always kept. It had a few photos, some letters, things like that. And there was this picture he showed me sometimes when he..." I swallowed, bile rising in my throat, but somehow forced the next words out. "...when he drank. His sister, Cassie. Cassie the witch. Willow Creek, Virginia. That's where he lost her, he said. Willow Creek."

A gust of wind shook the house. The elements of nature, trying to wash the darkest, most unnatural of magicks away from Willow Creek. I closed my eyes, felt fire tingle under my skin, like living lightning.

"And then you came here?"

I shook my head. "Not right away. After I aged out of the system, I wandered. I ended up in Savannah, working at a little tearoom. One of the other girls there, Ivy, was a witch too. On the January full moon, we did a spell. I saw Willow Creek. When I woke from the trance, somehow the photo of Cassie was in my hand. I knew I had to come here."

He set his mug down on the table. I wrapped my fingers around my mug, craving the warmth, the comfort of a cup of tea. Today was cold for a Virginia summer and rainy for pretty much anywhere.

But it wasn't the cold that got to me.

Aiden exhaled, giving his head a slight shake. "Is that why you wear the rose quartz? Because of the grief?"

My hand flew automatically to my necklace. I shrugged. "I don't know that I'm grieving Granddad anymore. Not most of the time, anyway. He had his troubles, and maybe now he's found peace. I don't know." I shook my head.

"It's okay if you are," Aiden said, the words matter of fact but not unkind.

The memory of that night seized me, threatened to pull me under and out to the sea of my past like a riptide. I'd told my friends and family in Willow Creek a lot about my past, but not...not everything about that night. I shook my head.

Granddad's words came back to me. They meant something. At the time, I hadn't thought them meaningful. I'd just been grateful for the chance to say goodbye. But if Willow Creek was teaching me anything, it was that nothing in my life was a coincidence.

A bit of movement in the backyard caught my eye.

"Crap," Aiden said, his mug once again hitting the table, this time with a thud.

The owl from last night landed in the yard. She gave the same call—one I was sure I'd know for the rest of my life.

Without thinking, I flung open the door, my feet already sliding into my ballet flats. They were hardly meant for walking in the rain, but who cared? This beautiful creature—perhaps, the familiar of the Guardian herself—needed assistance.

"Wait." Aiden walked beside me in long, quick strides, ducking his head against the rain. "What's it doing out here in the daylight? Owls are nocturnal."

"She paid me a visit last night," I said—as if that explained everything. "I guess she's just following up."

I knelt beside the owl, fighting the urge to reach toward her earthy-hued feathers. Her eyes pierced me with their intense gaze.

I reached out but didn't touch her.

"Careful," Aiden warned. "She's still a wild creature."

I held out my hand, tentative. "What do I call you?" I asked the owl. I couldn't call her "girl" or "sweetie." She was an owl, not a tortoiseshell cat, for the Goddess's sake.

The owl gave another pained cry.

Hoo-hoot-hoo-hoo.

And then she took off, the flapping of her wings surprisingly soundless.

I followed, running to keep up with her. She flew toward the woods. I didn't ask why. I only knew that I was meant to follow.

Vaguely, I heard Aiden call my name, but I didn't look back. We wanted answers, and here was the owl from last night? Hardly a coincidence. And I'd stopped believing in those anyway.

Aiden ran beside me, his movement effortless and graceful.

Once we reached the woods, following the owl became more difficult. We ran until my side ached, until my throat burned from exertion.

Before us, Willow Creek raged, its waters muddy and swift where they were usually clear and babbling.

The owl landed beneath a willow tree beside the banks. She walked beneath the draping branches, like an opera singer disappearing behind the stage's velvet curtains.

I peered under the tree, drawing back the leafy curtains to look for her. They were scratchy against my skin—nothing like velvet, I decided.

I frowned, turning to Aiden. "She's gone."

But his attention was focused on something on the other side of the tree. He shook his head. "I think her work is done for now," he said.

"What?"

He pointed. I followed the movement.

Before us, a doorway swirled. Made of tendrils of green and amber magic with hints of teal and flecks of gold, it beckoned.

A doorway to another world.

I stepped back, bumping into Aiden. "Where do you think it leads?"

He shook his head, seeming thoroughly engrossed in studying the portal. "Can't say. It reminds me..." He took a tentative step forward as if to get a closer look. "Of a painting a hedge witch in Oregon did. And hedge witches are experts in traveling between the realms."

"The realms?" I struggled to wrap my brain around that. I was still memorizing the healing properties of crystals and tending mint and basil on my windowsill. "You mean astral projection."

"Not quite. In astral projection, your body stays behind. This is a much higher level. You actually enter another realm."

"So, where does the portal lead?"

He shrugged. "I couldn't possibly say."

I kicked at the damp earth with my ballet flat, now soaked and covered with leaves and bits of grass, mud stuck in the grooves of the treads. "Great," I muttered.

"I say we go through."

"We don't know where it leads."

"My fox doesn't sense anything bad."

"I don't know what that means," I said. Also, I didn't know if I trusted his fox—not yet, anyway.

"The owl led us here for a reason."

I sighed. He had a point.

Aiden held out his hand.

"Do you have faith in magic?" he asked.

My heart pounded in my chest. I fingered the rose quartz pendant with my rain-soaked, sweaty fingers. "I..." I stammered but pressed on. "Of all the things in my life, magic is the one constant." There. I admitted it. Out loud. First time ever.

His outstretched hand waited: an invitation to another realm, an invitation to prove exactly how much faith I had in magic.

Droplets of rain dripped from his dark hair. His eyes were like twin flames on the stormy day. Behind us, the creek was a raging river.

"It's not a question of faith, Aiden," I said, dropping my rose quartz, hands falling to my sides. "The witches of Willow Creek are my family. I would do anything for them."

"Me too," he said, his voice soft and serious. I believed him.

I took his hand. We stepped toward the portal.

I wanted to step in tentatively, but as soon as we reached it, the energy drew us in.

We tumbled through a sea of colors. Magic brushed against my skin like ribbons of silk.

The only solid thing, in all of it, was Aiden's strong fingers gripping mine.

Despite the force of our fall, he never let go.

Aiden

My back hit solid earth. Before I could catch my breath, Vi crash-landed on top of me, hard enough that it took my breath away—not in some silly, romantic sense, either.

A raspy "oof" escaped my lips, even as my arms automatically wrapped around her. I was well aware, despite the disorientation of the fall, that we were in another realm of existence, some place magical. Not all magical realms were friendly—or technically open to witches and shifters passing through.

Vi sat up a little, her lower body pressing against mine. Her long hair had come loose from its braid in the fall, and soft waves of red hair framed her freckled face. I felt the goofy smile slide across my lips, but I'd chalk it up to the chaos of the fall.

Yeah. Sure. Simple as that.

She frowned. "Are you okay?"

I nodded, staring at her. I was all too aware of her body on top of mine, and though half of my brain said to get up and explore my newfound surroundings, the other half was much more interested in Vi, her body warm against mine, her green eyes made even greener by the dappled sunshine.

Her frown deepened. "What is it? Are you sure I didn't hurt you?" But she didn't move, though her gaze lifted to scan our surroundings.

I shook my head. "I'm fine. Really. A bit stunned. I thought it would be less of an Alice tumbling down the rabbit hole experience."

"Have you done this before?"

"Can't say I have. As a fox, I travel through the astral, but my body stays behind. But we're here. Mind, body, and soul. That's new for me."

She rolled off me and scrambled to her feet, offering me her hand. My inner fox made me pretty nimble on my feet, but I took her hand, a sizzle of warmth sliding through me as our fingers lingered.

Vi withdrew her hand from mine, but the memory of her warmth stayed. She balled up her hands in fists at her sides, as if ready for danger. I let my fox senses go on overdrive, trying to sense danger or threats afoot.

We stood in an ancient wood full of massive trees with gnarled branches and bright green leaves. Gleaming green moss dangled from the branches. Behind us, a tall but narrow waterfall cascaded into a silvery-blue pool. The water whispered of magic, as though it could wash cares away and make wishes come true. The sun shone here; its light filtered through the tree canopy.

I relaxed. "I think we're alone."

She glanced at me for a millisecond. "You *think*?"

"Fox shifter instincts," I explained. "I sense magic, though. Something wilder than witchcraft. It's old magic. Older than human magic."

"How do you know?"

I shrugged. "The fox knows things the man doesn't. His knowing is more primal, hard to put into words."

She nodded, a hint of tension dropping from her body—hands relaxing, shoulders dropping. "Why are we here? Where are we?"

"It's some place on the astral plane. A realm between realms, I think." I'd passed through the astral plenty of times during visions, but I knew through my study that there were these sort of hidden pockets within it where places like this existed. "It's a created place. Someone with powerful magic made this place."

"Through the power of imagination?"

"That. And a spell. A whole lot of old magic. Earth magic. Fire magic. Air and water, too. All of the elements, perfectly in balance." I turned to her. There was a peaceful quality to this place, a vibrant sort of stillness. "Do you feel it?"

She cocked her head. "I don't think I feel what you feel. This place feels unsettling to me."

"Huh." How could we have such opposite experiences? My fox wanted me to shift, to slink through the underbrush and hunt. The air was pure without a hint of pollution, only the scents of ferns, damp earth, pine, a bit of mushrooms, and a hint of something floral—violets, perhaps. No sounds of airplanes or tractors or cars, only birdsong and the rush of the waterfall, a tickle of breeze rustling the leaves of the deciduous trees.

The wind picked up, sending a spray of mist from the waterfall cascading over us. I shivered despite the warm air.

A woman's voice carried on the wind. It carried a hint of an accent that was hard to place—the British Isles, maybe Wales.

A keeper cries, a lost son dies.
A daughter learns, a son returns.
By fox and flame, by thorn of fae,
A secret revealed where night meets day.

The voice was beautiful, enchanting, but there was a sadness, a longing in it.

"Aiden," Vi whispered. "I don't like this place." Vi's face had gone white as a sheet. Her hand flew to the crystal at her neck.

I reached for her hand, squeezed it. I shouldn't have coaxed her into coming here. The riddle clue the woman gave was ominous to say the least—and not particularly helpful at this juncture.

"How do we help Evan?" I asked. "How do we save Willow Creek?"

Not yet. Again, a sort of pain in those words, a deeply rooted sadness.

When I blinked, Vi and I stood in the rainy forest of Aunt Ginny's farm, the swollen creek raging beside us.

Vi stared at me, her breath fast and shallow.

"Hey." I took her in my arms. We fit together like two puzzle pieces that belonged together. I held her against me. It seemed out of character, her trembling. "What did you sense there?"

Clearly, we'd had very different impressions. What had she sensed that I hadn't?

"It wasn't the place. The place was beautiful. Sort of like an enchanted forest from a fairytale. That part was lovely. It was just..." She drew away from me, wrapping her arms around herself and turning to face the creek. She exhaled before continuing. "I felt this surge of power, of energy. Of magic. Right before the woman's voice spoke to us."

"Like what?"

She shook her head. "Like something lost being found."

It hit me. "Something you lost? Your magic?" That didn't make sense. My inner shifter sensed Vi's magic immediately, her innate fire.

"Maybe." She tucked her humidity-frizzed hair behind her ear and turned to me. "I'm sorry. I have to go. I need to feed my cat her breakfast. She's gotten accustomed to a certain routine, you know?" She gave me a half-hearted smile that faltered and fell.

"Okay. I need to let my fox go for a run anyway."

"In the rain?" she asked.

I shrugged. "If the occasion calls for it."

I wanted to embrace her one more time, to brush away the stray strands of hair that still clung to her face. But she needed to run—as much, if not more, than I did.

"Do you want me to walk you back to the farmhouse?"

She shook her head. "No. I'm a country girl at heart. I can find my way through the woods blindfolded. Always been that way."

I watched her walk in long strides up the hill and disappear down the well-trodden path back to the house.

Only after I felt the tendrils of her fire magic disappear did I strip down and let the fox take over.

CHAPTER FIVE

Aiden

Why was the magic of that place so familiar? It was like a page from an illustrated storybook brought to life. Somewhere in mind, I was sure that image was tucked away in some long unopened drawer, waiting to be rediscovered. Or was it a dream, perhaps, one brushed carelessly away with the cobwebs of sleep upon waking?

I couldn't be sure of why that place felt so familiar and so vital—only that it wasn't done with me and Vi yet.

The fox longed to run, so I let him.

The rain fell in a steady mist, droplets collecting on my fur. The energy of the earth tingled beneath my paws. I sensed rabbits and squirrels, robins and crows, and a sleeping, hidden magic.

Where were the elementals? The gnomes of the earth, the sylphs of the air, the undines of the water, the salamanders of fire? It was as though they'd all gone into hiding—and a storm wouldn't be enough to drive such magical creatures underground.

No. There was a sulfuric tinge to the magic of Willow Creek these days, and it had something to do with what had happened to Evan, with what Evan and Nick's father was doing to the Guardian of the Crossroads.

When I'd had my fill of running, I curled up against a waiting tree trunk, a sturdy sweet gum that hummed with a gentle, creaking sort of energy.

Old one of the forest, my fox whispered, *tell me what you know. What secrets. What wisdom.*

A weary energy whooshed over me, tired, battered by storms and wind yet still standing.

"I've been here a century, wee one. Plus or minus a few years, but only the rings know for sure. And don't go asking, whatever you do."

I opened my eyes.

An old woman, her hair a tangle of moss and vines, sat before me on the damp earth. Vivid green eyes peered out from impossibly deep wrinkles.

She chuckled. "Let me guess, sly fox, you weren't expecting an answer?"

I shook my head sheepishly. "Can't say I was."

"Harrumph." She studied the dark gray sky above us, the unrelenting rain. "The earth is not happy, little fox. Shadows are threatening to choke us all."

"Is that why I'm here?"

She frowned at me, tracing shapes in the earth. Her skin was wrinkled, like bark, but covered in swirling, intricate tattoos reminiscent of vines. "Little fox, I don't know why you're here. Only what secrets I know, those that I can reveal."

I started to ask what those secrets were, only to catch myself in the nick of time. Whoever she was, she was a tree spirit, a nature spirit of some kind, perhaps the sweet gum itself, and meeting her was a rare blessing—one I didn't intend to squander. I inclined my head in a show of respect and deference.

With a heavy sigh, she began. "Once, long ago, the stories go, there were two sisters. They were of the fair folk, the ancient ones who walked this earth long before your kind. And when these fair sisters discovered the magic of Willow Creek—a sort of magical wellspring, if you will, where magical energy is continually renewed—they decided to share in its power."

Images flowed through my mind as she spoke. Both women were tall, one with hair the color of a newly kindled fire, the other with hair the color of freshly driven snow. One with eyes of emerald green. The other with eyes of smoky blue-gray. One with an owl at her side, the other with a raven. One wore a diadem of gold that spoke of birch branches, bedecked with delicate gemstones of rose quartz, purple amethyst, and blue lapis. The other, the one with the snow-white hair, wore a crown of silver studded with crystal points of smoky quartz, malachite, and tiger's eye.

The red-haired faerie was almost—*almost*—familiar. Her gauzy, emerald green dress swirled as she paced in a crystal-studded cavern, eyeing the other woman with suspicion.

"Ana-nene and Kalann, the sisters of summer and winter. Both tall and fierce and proud. One possessed of life and lightning, the other of shadow and frost. They shared Willow Creek equally—for a time. Ana-nene found love with a young human man, a farmer who worked the land. Though it lasted only a season, their union at Midsummer produced two sons—half-human, half-fae. But such a gift came with a price, for Kalann, the sister of winter's ice, already had a hard heart, and seeing her sister's delight with her twin sons left Kalann bitter."

The tree spirit shivered. "They say those winters that followed the boys' birth were the longest and coldest known in the history of Willow Creek. And then, when the boys turned thirteen—a magical age, as I'm sure a shifter would know—Kalann did a terrible thing. She kidnapped one of the boys, gave him a memory draught, and told him he was her son."

An image of the platinum-haired sister—her hair blowing the wind, her body clad in a navy wool clock embroidered with silver thread, her eyes burning with icy rage—flashed through my vision, and I shivered, longing suddenly for a warm fire and a pile of blankets.

The tree spirit nodded. "Ana-nene was furious. A battle ensued, not far from this very spot." She closed her eyes, leaning her head back. "An oak tree stood there, or so I'm told, for a time. Strange tree, one that wasn't one day and was the next. It was a tree, yet not a tree, a spell made solid for reasons we don't yet know. But that's another mystery.

"Ana-nene and Kalann fought, but they were equally matched. There, in those woods they lay, bloodied and battered, both gravely injured. And a young witch named Nettie came upon them. She took them to her farmhouse, and tended them, and healed them with her own remedies.

"After a time, Ana-nene confided in Nettie what her sister had done, and Nettie said she knew of Kalann's sorrow, for she, too, could not bear children, and her husband had left her, and now she tended the farm with her elderly parents, uncertain of her fate.

"After a season, the sisters healed, but their hearts were broken. Ana-nene found a safe place in the fae realm for her sons, and Kalann, now repentant, restored the child's memories.

"And, before the faerie sisters journeyed on to the faerie realm, they asked Nettie for a rather large favor. That the young witch would watch over the magical wellspring of Willow Creek—the Crossroads of Magic."

My heart pounded as the tree spirit spoke. Without knowing how, I was on my feet, fists clenched at my sides. "The Guardian of Willow Creek is human?"

The tree spirit shook her said. "No, lovie, not anymore. Not for a good many years. But she was, once, yes." She traced circles in the damp earth with her long nails. "Once upon a time, as the saying goes…"

"And the faerie sisters?"

The tree spirit's eyes, bright, nearly glowing green, locked with mine. "I can't rightly say that I know, little fox. Only that I feel a coming chill, though summer has scarcely begun, it seems. The elemental spirits have gone into hiding. Magic in Willow Creek is quiet and quivering. Who knows what the dawn will bring?"

The roar of my own blood filled my ears. My knees shook but I kept standing. This was so much bigger than any of us had imagined. "What—"

But it was too late. The tree spirit had vanished, leaving behind only the scent of moss and damp earth, and a faint green halo of earth magic where she had sat.

I knelt down where her fingers had traced the earth.

It was a series of spirals that reminded me of thorny vines.

Thunder rumbled overhead. I needed to get back to the farmhouse, to check on Evan and to tell Nick and Cassie what I'd learned.

Somehow, I dragged my exhausted, aching body back to the creek, where I tugged on my clothes. The image of Vi—her freckled skin, her quiet strength, her hair like sleek flames in that place that was and wasn't a place—wouldn't leave me anytime soon.

Vi

I pulled into my friend Bailee's driveway and cut the engine, clenching and unclenching my fingers on the steering wheel. A peculiar sort of magic tingled under my skin, making me feel almost agitated, a sort of restlessness.

Was it my time with Aiden and his shifter magic?

No. It had been that trip to the astral. I needed to understand what had happened. And Bailee wasn't just the librarian at the local public library. She was also a professional bookworm who had the best collection of magical books in Willow Creek.

I dipped my head against the misty rain and strode up the front porch steps.

Technically, the house belonged to her Grams, one of the Willow Creek Coven witches who was trapped on a mystical plane—if our suspicions were correct, one not nearly as pleasant as the one Aiden and I had visited.

The house was a pale blue Victorian with deep purple trim. The door was purple too. *A purple door means a witch lives here*, Bailee said mischievously the first night she had me over for tea, a windy and chilly night in late February shortly after my arrival in Willow Creek.

There'd been so much rain lately that the hydrangeas and rosebushes that encircled the house drooped toward the ground, their branches and blooms so heavy with rainwater. Even the earth herself seemed to sigh. *Will this weather never end?*

Me? I was more worried about what lay on the other side of this rotten weather—maybe now more than ever.

I raised my fist to knock on the purple front door, but it swung open before I could knock. Bailee stood there, her brown hair streaked with magenta, her teal cat's eyeglasses framing a face with impossibly long eyelashes and high cheekbones.

She quirked an eyebrow. "Everything okay? Evan?" I heard the telltale croak of her voice as it tightened around his name.

"He's fine. Well, the same." I winced as she ushered me inside.

She glanced away, but I saw her olive skin pale just a little.

Bailee had her own sense of style, and she wasn't afraid to show it off. Today, on her day off from the library, she wore a pair of black leggings with teal leg warmers and a long-sleeved magenta t-shirt that came to mid-thigh and was emblazoned with a black pentacle.

"You need tea," she quickly assessed and led me through a swinging door into a modern kitchen with vintage touches.

I tried to summon the courage to tell her why I was really here and not back home, curled up with Rosemary purring contently in my lap. But I was suddenly tongue-tied.

I had so many walls. Damned walls. I'd spent a lifetime building them, but lately? Sometimes I wanted to tear them down.

She put on the kettle and filled a teapot patterned with pale pink cabbage roses with plum-blueberry tea, casting a curious glance over her shoulder. "You're soaking wet," she said with a slight smirk.

Oh. I'd forgotten that. I tugged at my saturated shirt. "I was in the woods."

"Oh. Doing magic?" A glint of curiosity sparked in her eyes. Only once before had I met someone who leaned so fully into their magical being. My friend Ivy, back in Savannah.

"Walking." I turned away from the deepening curiosity in Bailee's gaze.

"Your energy is weird right now." Her tone wasn't mean. Far from it. She sounded concerned. "Vi?" She softened her voice. "You can tell me. Or not. But you came here for a reason."

The words rose in my throat but vanished before I could give them voice. I closed my eyes, squeezing them tight.

"Do you have any books about the astral realm?" Those weren't the words I meant to speak, but they'd do. Because if I was honest, I had feeling inside of me that had nothing to do with a quest for magical knowledge.

No. I wanted to know about Aiden. What kind of man he was. If he was who I wanted him to be.

Her eyebrow lifted slightly above her cat's eyeglasses, but she didn't give voice to her curiosity. She merely grinned. "Ah. If it's books ye seek, then ye've come to the right place."

I laughed. No one knew how to lighten a mood like Bailee Dugan.

She poured hot water in the teapot and placed it on a silver tray, along with two teacups and saucers, two demitasse spoons, and a jar of honey. "Come on. We'll have our tea while we scour Grams's library of witchery and magicks."

"Perfect. One second, though." I opened the fridge and examined the contents. I tended to be one of those people who ate constantly. In my defense, I was six-one, so my body needed a lot of fuel.

I found a plate of cucumber sandwiches waiting and grabbed those, along with a box of store-bought chocolate-chip cookies. Then, I followed Bailee upstairs to the bedroom turned library, where her grandmother, Tricia Dugan, kept her magical stores.

The scent of sage and magic swept over me as we entered the room. Beaded curtains framed the doorway, plum and navy beads held back by black wrought-iron tiebacks in the shape of dragon's claws. Black lace curtains filtered the gray sunlight, making the room with its sandy-hued walls and mahogany trim feel cavernous, so Bailee set the tray on a coffee table and flicked on the overhead light, a crystalline chandelier that sent tiny beams of light sparkling off polished bookcases and an old apothecary table.

My body relaxed every time I entered this room. It was a magical sanctuary, the energy holy, a place solely for magic in a hectic world.

Bailee sat on one of the two purple wingback chairs and poured the tea, adding a liberal amount of honey to mine. I polished off a handful of the mini cookies and several cucumber sandwiches and downed half a cup of tea.

"Wow. When's the last time you ate?"

"Who knows. I was at the farm all night, helping with Evan and...some other stuff came up."

Bailee's brows knitted in concern, her hands clasping in her lap. "Is he okay?" Evan and Nick were like brothers to Bailee, who had grown up an only child. I couldn't help but wonder if Evan was something more to Bailee. Or if maybe she wanted him to be.

"I didn't mean to worry you. He's fine. I swear. But we might be getting closer to having answers." I swallowed, taking another sip of tea, my throat now inexplicably tight.

She unclasped her hands and picked up her teacup. Thunder rumbled in the distance, and her gaze traveled to the gray world beyond the lace curtains, her lips, usually so eager to smile, twisted in a frown. "It's getting worse." She didn't mean the weather.

"It is. A magical storm is brewing." I took a sip of tea, the taste of tangy plums, tart berries, and sweet honey warming me. It was July, for the Goddess's sake. We should have been cranking up the air conditioner and sipping iced tea, not shivering in the rain. "Bailee, do you know Aiden McPherson?"

"Aiden?" She placed her cup, bedecked with an image of the Mad Hatter's tea party, on its matching saucer. "Yeah, I remember him. His brother too." Her tone darkened a little at the mention of Aiden's brother. "Tall, dark hair, kind of intense?"

I smiled. "Yeah, that's him. He's in town. And you know about his magic?"

She shook her head. "Only that his family had magic in their blood but wasn't too keen on it."

"So, you don't know he's a fox shifter?"

"Fox? Really?"

I nodded. "Do you know much about them?"

She stood, scanning the bookshelves that lined the room as if trying to remember. I knew that look. She was trying to find a book, searching her mental catalogue for its location. "Ah!" She walked over to one low bookcase, glass shelves supported by dark wood, goddess statues and crystalline spheres in hues of amethyst and onyx separating rows of books of various sizes and ages. She pulled one book off a shelf.

The Witch's Guide to Shifter Magicks, the black cover read in silver lettering. An image of a forest of green pine trees beneath a full silver moon and a smattering of gold stars also graced the cover.

Bailee ran a finger through the table of contents, then flipped to a page showing a black-and-white illustration of a fox.

"The fox shifter," she read, her voice taking on a lilting, breathy quality, "is known for his wit and cleverness. Highly resourceful, with a gift for thinking on his feet, the fox trusts his instincts to lead him in the right direction. In nature, the fox uses the magnetic fields of the earth in hunting their prey. Because the fox shifter embodies the qualities of the animal whose form he takes, he is deeply imbued with this magic, connected to the earth itself, to goddesses such as Gaia and Demeter, and to the fae and nature spirits. He is a journeyer, a seeker, much like the Magician of the tarot. And, like the Magician himself, he is one with a dual nature, though that duality within will often only be revealed to those closest to him. He keeps his secrets well. When a Witch encounters the Fox, the question she must ask herself is this: Is this particular fox shifter tricksy or trustworthy? Ultimately, the Witch must trust her intuition in her dealings with these creatures, even as she knows that not all foxes are the same, not all secrets are malicious, and no magic is purely of the light or of the shadow."

Bailee softly shut the book, but I continued to stare at the black cover.

Caught up in the spell of the book itself, part of me drifted back to the moment I toppled into the astral realm and landed in Aiden's arms. I couldn't hold in the words another second. I confessed my secret.

"Can you tell me?" I asked, squeezing my eyes shut.

"Tell you what?" Bailee asked. I heard her set the book on the table with an almost imperceptible thud.

"What kind of man he is?"

CHAPTER SIX

Vi

"Oh." Bailee leaned back in her chair, for once, speechless—and not much left my best friend at a loss for words. "I mean, I haven't seen him since I was a kid. But I remember we both loved books. We'd have these hour-long conversations about Tolkien, and his brother would call us nerds. Aiden and Liam were opposites."

I refilled my mug and inhaled the sweet scent of the now dark tea. "Like Nick and Evan?"

She shook her head. "No. Nick always resisted magic, like he feared it. And Evan really embraced it." Her voice quivered at those last words, but she forged ahead. "No. I just remember when Ginny would talk to us about magic, Aiden would lean in, like he was starving for every word—and committing it all to memory. Liam was...scornful. He looked down on all of us, the whole coven. He hated magic in a way no one I've ever known in the magical community hated it. Being around him was almost painful for me at times. Saint Nick, for all his faults, was never mean."

"I can't imagine how Liam and Evan got along."

She snorted. "They didn't. Liam was kind of a bully, and Evan always, always stood up to him. One time, Liam called me...well, he called me a fat dork. That sounds silly now, but I was ten years old. That was kind of a big deal to me then. And Evan shoved him into the swimming hole—hard, too." A smile flickered across her face, and I caught a glimpse of who Evan must truly be, of the person Aiden and I and everyone else were fighting so hard for. "Funny thing was, Liam called Evan about a thousand things ten times worse that day."

"He was defending his friend."

"Yeah."

"Why do you think Liam felt that way?" I couldn't help asking. He sounded like my grandfather in a way—terrified to the point of anger.

"His parents felt magic was a liability in the modern world. That it had a place in pre-industrial times, but in the modern world, with all of our technology, it had no use. And that it put the family at risk of...I don't know. Exposure, I guess? Scandal?"

"Huh. With my Granddad, it was all about it being a curse. Lots of superstition. He never cared about scandal."

"Maybe that's why you're drawn to each other. Something shared. Plus, you could use someone like Aiden—thoughtful, but with a playful side."

I polished off another cookie. "Are you saying I'm not fun?"

She laughed and tossed up her hands in a surrender gesture. "I did *not* say that."

She wrinkled her nose playfully. "What's he like now, anyway? I remember him when he was twelve and all gangly and awkward."

"Definitely not gangly and awkward," I said, swallowing, my throat dry. "It's like he sees everything, but he doesn't comment, you know? Like he's an observer."

"That part was true even when we were kids. He had this seriousness about him, but he was playful too. Different from Nick. Nick's always felt he had to be perfect, especially after his dad left. But Aiden, it's like he's a student of the world, and when he needs a break from pondering the universe, he plays."

"The dual nature of the fox?" I asked, taking a nervous swallow of tea.

"Sounds like it." She studied me. "You really like him," she pressed. It wasn't a question.

"We shared something…"

"Magical?"

I rolled my eyes. "In a very literal sense, yes. We followed an owl into the woods, and next thing we knew, we were on the astral."

"How do you know that's where you were?" She didn't sound skeptical, merely that curiosity again. I swear, if the woman hadn't become a librarian, she'd be a journalist.

"Aiden knew. I guess he's had some experience. He said the place we visited was a created place, filled with old magic." I crossed my legs, remembering the feeling of his arms around me. The man was under my skin, to be sure.

"Old magic? How old?"

I shook my head, my skin tingling. I could still feel that strange awareness coming over me, magic awakening, completely new. "Older than humans."

"Whoa. Like, the Goddess and God old? Like, the elementals? Faeries, maybe?"

"Faeries?" I hadn't thought of that. I knew the fair folk weren't all tiny little pixies, that they were powerful beings with magic humans could scarcely imagine. But I'd never encountered one. But the word sent that newfound magic crackling over my nerve-endings. "Could a faerie have built the place in the astral, the one that Aiden and I visited?"

"Well, if there's a book in Willow Creek that contains the answer, it's in this room."

I exhaled and rose, my knees knocking as I knelt to examine row after row of magical texts. Tricia Dugan's room of magic had everything a witchy woman like myself could ask for—an apothecary table full of oils, herbs, crystals, and candles. Athames and daggers and wands, chalices and a trio of cauldrons ranging from the size of an espresso cup to one as large as an average pumpkin. And, amid it all, the scent of magic swirled, like a bonfire on a moonlit night, like the lingering scents of candlewax and sage smoke, like spells and mystery, and the promise of what was yet to come.

After a good twenty minutes of searching, I stepped back from the last shelf. Bailee and I shook our heads.

"Nothing," Bailee groaned.

"Maybe she had a book about the astral realm, but hid it somewhere," I offered.

"Why would she do that?" Bailee stared out into the hallway, not meeting my gaze.

Something niggled at my gut. Was my friend hiding something? That was *not* a comforting thought, especially when dark magic was threatening our world.

"Tell me," I said, my voice more commanding than I'd intended.

Bailee met my gaze. "I've been searching for her, Vi." The words were laced with pained, an aching that washed over me. "Every night. In the world of dreams, I seek her. But I can't find her."

Tears filled her eyes, spilled over.

I hugged her. "I'm sorry. I shouldn't have pushed you. I know you're hurting."

Bailee sobbed. I felt like a complete jerk, demanding she spill her secrets. Using dream magic to seek your missing grandmother was far from a crime. I should've let her keep the secret to herself.

She pulled away, removing her glasses and swiping at her eyes. "How did you do that? I was determined I wouldn't tell anyone. It's like you compelled it out of me or something."

"I didn't mean to."

She forced a smile. "I know. Actually, it was weighing on me. Feels good to tell you."

Out in the hallway, the grandfather clock gave a single, lonely chime. One in the afternoon.

"Crap. I was supposed to be at the library at one. We have a permaculture class at two, and I want to be there to help set up."

"That's fine," I said. "I need to run home and check on Rosemary."

I sighed. No book. Nothing that could help us find Evan. "Bailee," I called as she headed toward her bedroom to change.

"Yeah?"

"We are going to find them—all of them. I'm going to do everything I can. The Willow Creek Coven is my family now." And, what I couldn't bring myself to say, was that meant everything to me—my magical family.

She nodded, swiping at her eyes. "I know. I should've told you I've been looking for Grams. And for a way to help Evan. But I haven't found anything. Not yet."

She hugged me again. "You seem different today," she said as we parted ways at the top of the stairs, my hand perched on the top of the mahogany banister.

I rolled my eyes. "Must be lack of sleep and too many cookies."

"No. There's..." Now she rolled her eyes. "I don't know. Something extra-mystical in your aura. Okay, maybe I'm the one running on too little sleep."

She gave me a wave and disappeared into her bedroom.

At the front door, I stared out in the rain, snakes of mist trailing along the ground. A shiver swept through me.

It wasn't right. So much of what was happening in our small, magical community wasn't right.

"Mother Goddess, give me the strength to make it right. May I bring back the sun, bring back the light. Balance the shadows, set magic right." The coven had been trapped for nearly a year. Evan was back, but not — not really. I couldn't help but feel that time was running out — that the storms were a message.

It was in the hands of the Willow Creek witches — those of us who remained, anyway — to stop Weylin Felson from destroying everything and everyone we loved.

Aiden

I lay there staring up at the ceiling of my van, my home on wheels for the last two years. When I'd started, I'd been looking for a true north, some distant pinprick of light to guide me home — wherever home was.

And all that time...I shook my head, my hair still slightly damp after the forest adventure. The walls of the van were covered in thin shiplap, layers of tapestries in various hues mixed with sparkling fairy lights. I had a small propane cookstove, a number of standard camping implements, a sleeping bag on a comfy mattress, and mementos of nature scattered through. A piece of driftwood from a beach in northern California. A conch shell from Key West. A few bits of sea glass, gathered on a rainy coast in Maine.

A journey of thousands of miles.

All to return here.

A light knock sounded at the back doors, and I cracked one open to see Cassie standing there in the gray light. Behind her, afternoon sun struggled to break through.

She smiled a worried smile. "Everything okay?"

I nodded. "Yeah. Needed a nap."

She studied me, this kind of sage, knowing look in her green eyes. "What are you thinking?"

I shrugged. I wasn't used to being asked so directly, and even when I was, I generally kept most of my thoughts to myself. "That soon enough, you'll be the one who guides us all."

She quirked an eyebrow. "Like a high priestess?"

I nodded. "Exactly."

She frowned. "That's Ginny's role."

"Cassie." I kept my voice low. There was a truth that needed to be spoken, but I didn't relish speaking it. "Change is coming. Upending everything. I don't know where we'll all stand when it's through with us."

Her lips parted, but she didn't waver, a flicker of resolve on her face. "We'll set things right. Isn't that why you're here?"

"I'm here for Evan," I pointed out. Except now I wasn't so sure.

"I just spoke to Vi and another sister-witch, Bailee. They're going to come over later and we can try some magic for Evan. Are you interested?"

"Of course."

She nodded. "Could you swing by Vi's? I thought, with your knowledge, you could help her sort through her crystals and herbs and see if you could find any that might work."

"I'd be happy to. I'll head over there now."

I hopped out of the van, catching her curiously peering inside. "What?" I asked.

She laughed. "I can't tell if hippies never went away, or if they're making a comeback."

I couldn't help my amused chuckle, seeing the van through her eyes—as a time traveler from the 1970s. "A bit of both, Cass."

As I circled toward the front of the van, Cassie made her way to the chicken coop, where Nick was throwing feed to the birds. She greeted him with a kiss, and his arm looped briefly around her waist.

A woman's voice drifted through the ether, a scent of oakmoss and musk and amber carrying with it. My hand paused over the driver's side door handle.

Questing fox and lost daughter,
Sacred rose and roving son,
Where summer fire meets autumn air
A bit of magic comes undone.

I had no idea what it meant.

The memory of Vi's body crushing against mine in the astral rose up again.

Somehow, this quiet witch and that mystic place were pieces of a puzzle that would tell me what I'd been searching for.

Maybe it wasn't just Willow Creek, my family's farm, and my cousins I was coming home to.

Vi

I curled my legs underneath me and sank deeper into the sofa. It was a soft velvet loveseat in a faded olive color. I'd found a couple tapestries in a bin at the local thrift store and sewn my own throw pillows, one of which cushioned my back. Rosemary Caterwaul Broomsticks sat on another cushion beside me, leaning her head into my hand as I scratched behind her ear. Her purr was the sweetest kind of music.

The walls of my apartment above the Piper Street Co-Op, where I worked most afternoons and evenings during the week, were brick long since painted white, and the windows were tall and wide, letting in lots of light, though I'd added some tapestry-sewn curtains for privacy.

I'd set my rose quartz pendant on the windowsill in a circle of selenite and clear quartz. The selenite cleansed the rose quartz, and the clear quartz amplified the cleansing vibrations of the selenite.

I sipped a cup of cinnamon-black tea with honey, leaning my head against a throw pillow, this one navy blue with mustard-yellow flowers and olive-green vines.

I'd thought I would take a nap and grab some food before prepping my herbs and crystals for a ritual to help Evan tonight. I'd demolished a grilled cheese and tomato sandwich and a half a bag of sweet potato chips, but the nap wasn't going to happen. I felt too on edge.

The trip to the astral. Aiden's sudden appearance—and my inability to stop thinking about him. The strange magic stirring under my skin, like some new power awakening. It was creepy.

Bailee's revelation didn't help. My best friend had been journeying in her dreams, searching for her Grams. That kind of thing sounded risky. Worse, she sounded desperate. And Bailee was usually so full of joy and optimism.

And I couldn't shake the sense that with every gust of wind, every clap of thunder, every bolt of lightning, we were careening toward some precipice of dark, shadowy magic.

A knock sounded at the door. I set Rosemary on her pink cat bed, but she jumped out, circling my feet and rubbing her face against my ankles instead.

"Who's there?"

"It's Aiden." There was a pause, then, "Cassie asked me to swing by. To help with the stuff for the ritual tonight."

The sound of Aiden's voice grounded me the way few things could these days—and I wouldn't explore that realization. I opened the door, my breath hitching slightly. He'd changed out his rain-soaked clothes from that morning and currently wore a pair of black linen pants that seemed designed for yoga or tai chi, and a grayish-blue shirt with a tree of life emblazoned on the front. I couldn't help studying him, there in the threshold to my apartment, as I recalled what Bailee had told me about him and what she'd read about fox shifters.

But it was the memory of his arms around me in the astral forest that made heat pool in my belly.

"Vi?"

I shook my head, my cheeks heating. "Sorry. You caught me at a bad time. I was really immersed in my book."

Unable to sleep but needing to stop pacing, I'd grabbed a favorite fantasy read off my shelf. It currently sat facedown, open to my current page on the sofa.

He frowned, the picture of politeness. "Sorry. I can come back."

"No. Come in." I ushered him inside the apartment. Rosemary sauntered closer, sizing him up. I glanced at my cup of tea and the copy of *The Dark is Rising*. I toyed with my hair in its braid. "I'll fix you some tea."

"That would be nice."

He stepped in, and I caught his eyes taking in the place. I stepped into the small kitchen. The water in the electric kettle was still hot. I filled a tea ball with a fire magic tea blend—orange peel and cinnamon made up the backbone of this particular blend.

I handed the mug, bedecked with a pattern of woodland creatures, to Aiden. "Cream or sugar?"

He shook his head. "Black is fine. Smells amazing."

"It's one of my favorites."

"You have a gift for tea blends. I bet when you do open your shop, it will be packed every day."

I laughed and sipped my tea, settling onto the sofa. "Maybe someday. The owner of the Piper Street Co-Op downstairs sells some of my blends, and I have an online shop. That's enough for now. I work at the co-op during the week, and that pays the bills. My life in Willow Creek is more than I'd ever hoped for."

He sipped his tea, leaning back on the sofa, his body angled toward me, long legs stretched in front of him. A copper necklace with a large square pendant of polished green jasper at his throat caught my eye. It called to me, that hunk of stone.

Or was it the man who wore it?

"In what way?" he asked.

"What?"

"You said your life in Willow Creek was more than you'd ever hoped for. I just wondered in what way."

"Oh." I set my mug down on the steamer trunk that doubled as a coffee table. "Well, I get to practice magic openly. I have a coven now. And I have a home of my own. I mean, my foster mom was amazing—is amazing, actually—but this place is mine, you know?"

He nodded. "I understand that. My parents hate magic, and I was expected to suppress mine."

I bit my lip, remembering Bailee's words. Should I ask for more details? I mean, he'd brought it up. "How would you suppress shifter magic? Is that even possible?"

A bit of tea sloshed over the side of his cup. I reached out to steady his hand. The color left his cheeks, and I recognized the hollow pain in his eyes for what it was—trauma.

I took the mug from his hand and set it on the table. I took his hand in mine, squeezing it, unable to stop myself. "If you want to tell me, you can. I'm good at keeping secrets."

His amber eyes met mine. He cleared his throat. Slowly, he turned his palm upward, squeezing my hand. "I want to tell you, Vi. There is a way to suppress a shifter's powers. A potion that might as well be poison. It suppresses our powers, but at a terrible price."

I could tell by his tone he wouldn't take such a thing voluntarily. "Goddess, Aiden. They didn't make you...?"

He nodded. He was shaking now.

I drew him against me. How could this man, this strong, wise fox, be so wounded by the people who were supposed to love him?

Was this how Cassie felt, all those years ago, when she fled her family seeking freedom?

He pulled away from my embrace, the movement slow but deliberate. "That's my secret," he said with a faltering smile. "What's yours?"

I shook my head. "I don't know where to start."

His thumb slid over mine, and then up my wrist. The movement was simple, but the effect was hypnotic.

I tilted my head back and closed my eyes. For a moment, I wanted to lose myself in him, in the way I felt when he was near. I could imagine him undressing me, those lips all over my body, those amber eyes dark like embers with passion...

He squeezed my hand. "If you want to share anything, you can." His voice sounded constricted, pained, as though his throat were tight.

I opened my eyes.

"When I was thirteen, I saw my grandfather's ghost," I blurted out. I tugged my hand out of his grasp and turned away, wrapping my arms around myself.

"His ghost?"

I nodded. "The night he died. His ghost came to me. His spirit. He said he was sorry he didn't do better. And he said...He said the strangest thing." Silence, as Aiden listened, seeming to take in every word. "That he didn't know where I got my red hair from. 'Must've been your daddy,' he said. I never got why that's the last thing he thought of, why that was one of the last things he said to me. We never talked about my father—ever. It wasn't important who he was, Granddad said, because it wasn't like my dad was ever around. It's weird, right? It's a weird thing to say."

I stopped talking, realizing I was rambling.

Aiden gazed down at me, his expression kind yet thoughtful. "Maybe it wasn't weird or random. Maybe, as he crossed from our realm to the realm of the dead, he learned something."

"About my father?"

Aiden rubbed the back of his neck. "I saw something in the forest today after you left." He inhaled deeply and began a long story, about faerie sisters and wild magic. My heartrate increased with every word.

After he'd finished his tale, his eyes met mine. "Maybe what your grandfather realized was that you are, indeed, a witch. But maybe he learned that you're something more, too."

My breath caught, fear washing away all other emotion. Because something inside of me said yes, that was true. And for some reason, that scared me. "I'm not. I'm me, okay? I'm a witch. Plain and simple."

He frowned. "There's nothing plain or simple about being a witch."

The lights flickered, no doubt the storms rolling through.

"What else would I be, then?" I asked.

The lights flickered.

Off. On.

Off. On.

Off. On.

Oh, Goddess. Was I causing that? My magic, spinning out of control?

"It's all right," Aiden said. "I didn't mean to upset you." His voice was soothing, but rough with worry.

I reached for my rose quartz, too late remembering I'd set it on the windowsill. My fingers instead clutched a wire-wrapped tiger's eye stone I'd chosen instead. Courage, it was supposed to represent.

But the energy was simply too much.

The lights wouldn't stop flickering. I closed my eyes and covered them, the flaring of lights on and off too much to bear.

"Tell me what you mean," I demanded. I never made demands. Ever. Goddess, what was with me today? There was force in my words.

Rosemary shoved her head under my hand, as if to demand that I take comfort in her presence. A true-blue witch's familiar, if there ever was one. I soaked in her comfort, and the comfort of Aiden's presence, his gentle, thoughtful energy.

I opened my eyes, too agitated to keep them closed. The room was dark now, only the dim light of the rainy day lighting the room.

Aiden knelt beside me, petting Rosemary but that concerned expression on his face directed at me. "I think you might be part fae."

CHAPTER SEVEN

Aiden

Magic filled the room, smelling of a forest damp with rain, like mushrooms and mist and wildness. My inner fox perked his ears. Wisps of crimson and gold magic swirled, half-witchy, half-something else. Something like what I'd sensed in that enchanted forest in the astral realm.

This magic? It was half-human, half-otherworldly.

"Hey?" I kept my voice soft, kneeling beside Vi. She covered her face with her hands. "What's happening right now?"

"Do you think he knew?"

I sat on the floor beside her. Vi's cat, a tortoiseshell with vivid green eyes much like her mistress's, curled into her touch. Vi caressed the cat's short fur.

"I don't know," I said. "Sometimes, as spirits cross from the realm of the living and make their way through the veil, they see things. Secrets are revealed." I did my best to project calming energy toward her. I'd known my whole life I was a shifter, just as she'd known that she was a witch. And now she'd learned that maybe she was part fae. What must she be feeling?

She nodded, as if processing this information.

"It's just a theory," I hurriedly added. "The whole faerie thing."

"But I think you might be right." She'd withdrawn her hands from her face. The magical energy still filled the room, but it was calmer now, like a gust of wind becoming a gentle breeze. Still, the wild, ancient energy tugged at me, drawing me in. Anyone with magic in their blood would be drawn to it, but for me, a fox shifter, it was especially tempting.

She stood. "I should learn more about it. I mean, does it have anything to do with why I'm here, in Willow Creek? I thought I came to find Cassie, but what if someone—or something—brought me here."

"It's possible." I stroked my chin, remembering. "I met a faerie witch in New Hampshire—a witch who'd pledged her magic to working with the fae. She was born in 1850 but doesn't look a day over thirty. She's spent a lot of time in the faerie realm, and because time passes differently there, she hasn't aged like most humans do. I spent three weeks helping her tend her faerie garden.

"She made the best tea—well, not as good as yours. She said the fae are masters of many things—of magic, of the healing powers of the plants and earth. A faerie can make anything grow, she said, and knows how to use every plant for the greatest good or greatest ill. The world sings to them, and they can travel many planes of existence, never losing their way. And they can also use those songs to call objects through the veils that separate the realms. A teacup or a dagger, she said, can be drawn from one realm to another."

Vi's face was entranced. We were both students of magic, and an image flashed in my mind of the two of us on a rainy autumn night, a pot of tea and two teacups on the table next to stacks of open books.

I swallowed. I'd thought I'd spend my whole life wandering—or running. Some strange mixture.

What if there was another option?

She stayed silent, so I pressed forward. "I don't know if you have faerie blood in your veins or not. But I do know that if you do, it's a gift, something to be celebrated, not feared."

Her fair skin was even paler than usual, her freckles standing out against high cheekbones. Her green eyes were somber, seeming to change color. Right now, they reminded me of the silver sage that grew in Flora, the faerie witch's, garden, that pale green with a hint of gray.

Vi reached toward her neck, then frowned and glanced at the window. She walked toward the window, where she plucked her rose quartz pendant off the sill and fastened the silver chain around her neck. "What if that power is awakening? What if it's awakening and I don't know how to control it? And why? Why now?"

I shook my head. "I don't know." I crossed the room toward her. I couldn't stop myself. I took her hand in mine, waiting for her to pull away. She leaned closer.

Both parts of me, the fox and the man, reacted. She smelled like magic and moonlight, like a wild forest and a meadow of violets. "Not yet. But we'll find out."

Vi's lips flickered into a smile. "You study everything, don't you?"

"If it interests me enough."

"Are you studying me right now?"

"Yeah."

"What have you learned?" The question was surprisingly bold.

I didn't flinch in the face of it. "That you are kind. That you are loyal. That you've embraced your magic, endured hardships. And that, although you have fear, you don't let it stop you. You leaned into your magic. You started a life here in Willow Creek. You've forged a bond with a new coven. All of that takes courage."

With her free hand, she cupped my chin, her thumb rubbing my jaw, still covered with a thin layer of stubble.

"I want to be courageous," she whispered. "I'm worried my stores are dwindling when I need them most."

"Impossible," I whispered back.

I couldn't be sure who kissed who. It wasn't a long and deep kiss, but something soft with a promise of more.

When we drew away, I could see by the light in her eyes she wanted more, just as I did.

Witch or fae or some combination, Vivienne Gearhart was quickly weaving a spell around me. If I kissed her again, where would it lead?

Sweet Goddess.

I cleared my throat, desperate for distraction. "The question is, how does all of this tie together? It's like all of our destinies led us here, to this place, this moment."

Vi rubbed her fingers over the polished bit of rose quartz on its silver chain. "I agree. None of us is here by coincidence. And we can't sit around waiting for the pieces to fall into place." Her voice dropped lower, deepening with worry as she spoke. "There's one place that holds the answers. And I think it's up to the two of us to go there."

"That place in the astral? I don't think I could find my way back there if my life depended on it."

Vi shook her head. "The owl—the Guardian's familiar—led us to that portal. So, maybe we don't go to the astral forest. Not first, anyway. We start somewhere else. The Crossroads of Magic."

The Crossroads. Where magic was born into this realm. The place the faerie sisters had entrusted the Guardian to watch over all those years ago. "How do we get there?"

"You said the fae can journey between the realms of existence, right?"

"Yeah, but..."

"Well, isn't the Crossroads one of those realms? And as a shifter, you can journey as well."

"You don't know how to control your fae gifts—and that's really just an untested hypothesis at this point. It could be dangerous. We don't know what or who is waiting for us down there."

"I agree. Look, I'm not the sort to go charging headlong into danger. But Evan is clearly suffering, and there's this dark magic in the air. We all feel it." She speared me with her gaze, green eyes intense. "Tell me you don't feel it."

I stood. "You know I feel it. It crawls against your skin like fire ants waiting to bite."

"I'm not going to stand by and watch everyone I love be hurt by that darkness. We have to fight."

"The two of us, alone?"

"When Nick and Cassie went, Bailee and I served as their anchors in this world. But you and I don't need that because we can traverse the realms at will."

I raked my fingers through my hair, sighing. "That simple, huh?"

"Yes." Her soft whisper suggested it was anything but simple. We both knew the risks. Perhaps, Vi knew them more than I did.

But it was Evan's anguished spirit that drew me to this place. I couldn't let him suffer any longer. Nick told me last night Evan had been down in those Crossroads, a prisoner, for nearly a year.

I squeezed Vi's hand. "How do we begin?"

Vi

I carried a box of crystals out from the bedroom. It was an old jewelry box I'd found at a local antiques place. I'd smudged it with sage and blessed it, then lined it with black felt and placed my crystals inside. My smaller, to-go box was still back at Nick and Cassie's farm, in case they needed those stones for Evan.

I set the box on the floor between Aiden and me, inhaling sharply as the magic hit me. The energetic vibrations of the crystals rippled across my skin—some of them light as a breeze, others fiercely protective like rolling thunder, still others tugging me toward the earth with their grounding, stabilizing energy.

I ran my hand over the waiting crystals without touching them, just sensing their energy, letting my intuition guide me. It had taken me years to trust that instinct.

But if I could learn to trust my intuition when it came to crystals, tarot, and tea blends, why not other things? Why not a long-forgotten faerie magic, ready to reawaken?

I tucked that thought away for another time, letting the crystals' magic flow through me.

One drew me in, a tingling, pulsing feeling vibrating through my palm and fingers as they passed over it. I picked it up. An airy, almost dreamy sort of energy washed over me. It was at once energizing yet calming.

Aiden sat beside me on the floor in simple cross-legged pose. Rosemary was curled up on his lap, staring up at him like she was in *L-O-V-E love*.

I held the crystal out for him to inspect. "Ametrine."

He nodded. "I've heard of it. It's used for astral travel."

"I didn't know that. But it makes sense. The woman at the shop said it combines the spiritual insight of amethyst with the will and ability to manifest of citrine. I'd imagine successful astral travel is a combination of both insight and manifestation." I'd picked this particular polished stone up on a trip to Roanoke with Bailee, at her favorite crystal shop there, drawn to the purple hue with its hints of orangish gold. I set the stone on the floor beside me.

The woman at the shop had said something else, a keen knowing in her eyes as she watched me roll the stone in my palm. *It unites male and female energy.*

But I couldn't voice those words. Because the thought of my energy and Aiden's, combined? It made an ache pool at the apex of my legs; one I knew only he could satisfy.

Aiden rubbed behind Rosemary's ears, and she leaned back, purring. "You know your crystals," I said, desperate to forget that ache. "Is that something you learned on your, uh, travels?"

He nodded, his words thoughtful. "I've dabbled in a lot of things. Healing magicks, crystals, herbal lore, astral projection. Mostly, anything magical that relates even tangentially to my shifter magic. I'm almost always restless—unless I have a good book in my hands. Then I'm on the journey of a lifetime and time slips away."

Sweet Mother. Who was this man, and which blessed love goddess had dropped him into my life? The heat did *not* dissipate.

He frowned. "What?"

I shook my head. "I've always felt the same way. For different reasons, though. I'm not much for restlessness. I craved roots. But books, they always feel like home. The world disappears. There's a magic in that."

He nodded. "Exactly." He leaned over and studied my collection of gemstones and crystals. He started to reach out, then quickly curled his fingers in, as though stopping himself. "I'm sorry. Do you mind if I...?"

"Be my guest."

His eyes took in the stones, and I knew he wasn't just seeing their colors and shapes—a point of titanium quartz with its rainbow hues, a polished heart of purple amethyst, a strand of carnelian beads in deep rusty orange, polished pieces of everything from tiger's eye to ocean jasper to snowflake obsidian.

His gaze fixated on one stone that was, at first glance, a mere rock. It wasn't a precious gem or a crystal. He picked up the white stone, testing its weight in his palm.

"A hag stone," I said.

"Also called a faerie stone."

"I didn't know that. To me, they're hag stones or holey stones. My friend Ivy gave it to me. She found it as a young girl on a trip to Germany with her family. She said she'd always known it was meant for a friend, and that I was that friend."

"She sounds like a very intuitive person."

"She is. And wise, yet a little naïve at the same time." A feeling of worry tugged at my gut. She'd sounded a bit down the last time we talked. She'd had an argument with her mom, she said, which was odd because the two of them were super close.

Aiden closed his fist around the hag stone—or faerie stone. Another wave of magic rippled through the air, and a green and amber aura of magic radiated out from around the stone.

"Crap!" Aiden dropped the stone like it was on fire. The stone clattered to the floor. Rosemary took off, disappearing into the bedroom.

The wave of magic faded, leaving only a lingering aroma of damp earth, fresh rain, and moss.

I picked up the stone.

"Careful. It's hot," Aiden warned.

"No." I balanced the small white rock on my palm. It looked like a nondescript river rock—except for the three holes that the forces of nature had bored into it. To my touch, it was cool.

I tilted my head. Its energy felt new, a quivering against my palm. "Why is it called a faerie stone?" I asked. Even to my ear, my voice sounded strangely dreamy.

"It's said that looking through the hole in the stone can allow a witch to see into other realms—most commonly seen is the faerie realm, thus the name. And, if a witch finds herself or himself in the realm of the fae, the stone can guide them back, like a compass pointing toward home."

I couldn't help it. The stone's energy began to call to me, like a sweet, melodic chant in a language long lost. It spoke of meadows of wildflowers of too many varieties to name, forests of impossibly tall trees, wild streams of rushing water tumbling over rock.

"Vi, your magic feels really...charged right now," Aiden said. "I don't know if you should."

"We need answers," I said. I handed him the ametrine. "I think we found...not an answer, exactly. But a key to a locked door. And maybe the answer is behind that door."

I held the hag stone up, magic swirling along my skin. Amber wisps of magic radiated from me, meeting the green aura of the stone.

I grabbed Aiden's hand.

My heart raced, and a knot formed in my belly.

"Be careful," Aiden said, his voice low. "Please."

He was right. What was I doing?

A cry in my head—Evan's. Another storm. More magical torment. "It's not for me, Aiden." For myself, I wouldn't take such a risk.

"For Evan, then?"

I nodded. "That's why you're here, isn't it?"

"I thought so."

"And not just Evan. My best friend, Bailee. Her grandmother is trapped in the same magical realm where Evan was held. And for Nick and Cassie. They've sacrificed so much, risked their lives. Nick's grandmother and mother are out there somewhere. An entire coven of witches. We have to—for them."

Aiden seemed to consider this. After a long pause, he nodded. "Yes."

The magic was building, throbbing, pulsing. My head ached with it.

I squeezed Aiden's hand. His amber eyes met mine, a resolve in his that matched my own.

"If the question is, what would I do for them, you know what the answer is?" I leaned forward, uncharacteristically bold. "Anything."

I raised the stone to my eye. My amber magic mixed with his mossy green earth magic. I looked through the hole in the stone.

If I'd been expecting to catch a glimpse of another realm—some crystalline pool, or a wood elf on the hunt for a prized stag, or an iridescent unicorn—I was in for one nasty surprise.

I glimpsed a swirling vortex of rainbow hues, surrounded by inky pools of shadow.

The shadows took shape, almost like hands made of an oil slick. They looped around us and tugged us down before a scream could even leave my throat.

CHAPTER EIGHT

Aiden

The force of the fall ripped my fingers from Vi's impossibly strong grasp.

I opened my mouth to shout, but our free fall, combined with some sort of mystical gale-force wind, stole the sound.

My stomach felt lodged in my throat. And my heart? Nothing, like I was trapped in the pause between beats.

I slowed — not of my own volition — and met earth that was a mix of spongy and rough. Moss. A thick, cushy carpet of moss.

I blinked. Above me, no longer the high ceiling of Vi's apartment. And not sky, either, like in that astral forest. Instead, high above us, root systems tangled in dark earth. Crystal points dotted the labyrinth of roots. Silvery moss dripped from those roots, reminding me of live oaks with moss back home.

"Wow." Vi's voice greeted me. I rolled to one side, managing to prop my head on my elbow despite the lingering vertigo.

"That wasn't freaky at all," I grumbled.

Vi turned to me, her hair splayed over the bed of moss that had cushioned our fall. A glance around me told me that everywhere else in this subterranean place was mostly dark, glittering points of jet and onyx, cold-looking slabs of dark granite, and bare earth. A few patches of flowers and vines, sure. But soft beds of moss? Not so much.

Vi reached for my hand. "At least we had a lucky landing."

"Hmm." Something felt off. "Too lucky?"

"What do you mean?"

"I don't know." Not yet. Except that we already had too many mysteries to solve. Why bother trying to figure out the Case of the Mysterious Landing?

We should stand. But I didn't want to stand. Because Vi's fingers were intertwined with mine, her touch warm and soft. And the way her deep red hair framed her face, the smattering of freckles across her nose and cheeks...not to mention that bit of freckled skin I could see on her chest. I swallowed. Her green eyes seemed darker down here, lending her a sense of mystique that reminded me of the endless forests of the Pacific Northwest.

She smiled, squeezing my hand and wrinkling her nose. "What are you thinking?"

"That this bed of moss that cushioned our fall seems a bit out of place."

"It's the Crossroads of Magic," Vi pointed out, sitting up, glancing around. "We don't know what is possible down here."

"True enough." My fox felt it before my human side, the magic sliding over me. Part of it was pure energy, vibrating at a higher, lovelier frequency than I'd ever felt. But I felt an undercurrent of shadow here, too.

My own magic—shifter magic—burned full-force inside of me.

In that moment, my father's voice came to me. It was the eve of my sixteenth birthday, and he'd offered me a Mercedes—brand new, fresh off the assembly line—if I agreed to take the potion that would suppress my shifter side.

"You are not a fox," he'd said, his voice stern, an anger seething beneath the surface. "You are a man. Maybe, you could be a good man." He'd left the vial on my dresser.

Every moment of defiance? Every refusal? Every time I embraced the shifter magic a bit more? With every shift, I'd moved closer to this moment.

Vi knelt beside me. Her hair had come undone from its loose braid in our fall. It cascaded in waves around her face, its color somewhere between tiger's eye and garnet. "About the moss…"

I shifted against the mossy bed, waiting for its moisture to seep through my clothes. It didn't. Huh. Just…huh. I inhaled sharply. Her magic, my magic, tumbling together…

"What about it?" I managed to ask.

"I think it was me."

"You planted this moss here?" My own voice sounded strained to my ears. In the reverberating magic of this place, my fox knew what my human side denied. It was something he'd known, perhaps, that day long ago, when he'd sensed what I now knew was Vi's magic.

But I couldn't say it aloud. Not yet.

She swept her hair over her shoulder, where it toppled across her chest. It was the magic of this place, drawing me to her. Fox to witch. Or was it fox to fae?

I shook my head, sitting in a simple cross-legged pose, as her words dawned on me. She wasn't speaking in hypotheticals.

"On the way down, I was thinking, *I hope we land somewhere soft. Maybe some moss or something,*" she said.

"Well, we came here looking for answers. And that would be a faerie ability. I didn't expect it so quickly, but this place is very much aligned with the fae. So, in a way, that seems reasonable."

She laughed. "You act like it's the most normal thing in the world."

"In our world, what is normal?" I said.

A chill settled over me, the initial warmth fading. We both stood, rubbing our arms.

She gave a visible shiver. "There's a dark, quiet beauty here, don't you think? It's cloaked in something out of place, but you can still sense it. I think this is it—the place where Cassie and Nick found Evan. I think we made it to the Crossroads of Magic."

Vi

Silver mists snaked along the ground. The Crossroads of Magic. It was just as Cassie had described it, except a million times more eerie.

Above us, multi-colored roots tangled in dark earth. They glistened in the hues of all the elements—the mossy green of earth, the golden hues of the sunny air, the deep blue of a crystalline pool, the crimson of the flame. Crystal points jutted out among the knotted roots, just as colorful.

My fingers flew to the rose quartz at my throat. Only last night, it had been hot against my skin, like the memory of stardust nestled between my collarbones.

It was cold now, like a dull, hollow ache.

"Something is wrong," I said.

"Well, we did fall through a portal. And we don't exactly know that the faerie stone will take us home. So, I'd say so."

I shook my head. "No. Don't you feel it? The magic here is...sick. Tainted."

Aiden tilted his head. His inky hair was mussed from our fall, his bright, warm eyes squinting into the lurking shadows—the fox, seeing what normal humans could not. His face paled, tension seizing his shoulders. "It reminds me of something—the potion. The one my dad made me..." He stopped himself, his Adam's apple bobbing as he swallowed. "I don't think this is meant to suppress the magic, though, like the potion did. It's almost like..."

"A curse?" I supplied.

He nodded.

The cold of this place swept over me—no, through me. "I can't shake the feeling we're standing on a precipice," I said. "It's been almost a year since the shadow magic took the coven. And then Evan came back, but he's not back—not really. The owl's visit to me last night. Her guiding us to the portal this morning. Your vision that brought you to Willow Creek. Our journey on the astral. It's like..." My lips couldn't form the words, couldn't give voice to a thought that frightening.

"Like whatever is being planned by whoever is planning it, it's about to happen." Aiden finished the thought for me.

I glanced at him. He had courage but wasn't foolhardy. Like the fox, he was clever, a blend of mystic energy and earthy practicality. If I allowed myself to be truthful, wasn't he the sort of man I'd once hoped for? Thoughtful, kind, strong, dependable. And bonus points for hotness and a sense of humor.

No. Not going there. Not now.

"I wish I had my tarot cards," I said. "They could give us some guidance on our next steps."

"Maybe we have to trust our intuition."

"That's never come easily to me. The cards are what help me connect to my intuitive side. To give voice and shape and form to the whisperings of my magic."

"Well said," Aiden said. "You know, you conjured the moss. Try conjuring a tarot deck."

"I'm not sure that's how it works." I laughed, a shaky, nervous sound like a bell's rusty jangle. "Okay, so I don't have a clue how it works. Or if it works. The moss thing could've been a coincidence. Or not me at all."

Could I even do something like Aiden suggested? Yesterday, I'd have dismissed it outright.

Today, everything had changed.

"No. I saw it in you from the moment our eyes first met. You have the most powerful magic I've ever encountered, Vivienne."

He moved toward me, bridging the distance between us. My legs felt like gelatin, weak and wobbly. He leaned down, brushing my hair behind my ear. His stubble tickled my cheek as his lips hovered scant millimeters from my earlobe. "You have the wildest, deepest magic I've ever known. We are going to break this fucking curse." He leaned back, smiling, in that moment the sly fox.

His husky murmur promised more than just victory.

My skin flushed hot despite the dank, cold air. Sweet earth mother. How long had I waited for someone like Aiden McPherson?

And the hunger I felt rising in me? I saw it reflected in his eyes, burning, molten pools of amber.

"Aiden..."

"Soon." There was an ache in his voice that hadn't been there before. "Soon," he repeated, his voice a rough, yet soft, growl.

I nodded, sucking in a few grounding breaths of musty air.

A shiver slithered up my back. The air felt heavy now, as though it stirred, sentient, sensing us. Hadn't Cassie said the fog here seemed to have a mind, a presence of its own?

"Aiden?"

"I feel it." His gaze was sharp, as if taking in any and all potential threats in our environment, the spell of our desire broken for the time being.

The shadows seemed to encroach, sensing our presence. Something about us was clearly a threat. A sickly magic slithered over my skin, like stepping into a cobweb.

The shadows growled.

Aiden shoved me behind him.

"No." I stepped in front of him. If I did possess some fae lineage, that could give me some sort of immunity against whatever foe we faced. If I could conjure something from thin air, that could be exactly what I needed.

The shadows coalesced into a shape. Twisting and writhing, forming muscle and sinew, bone and claw, they took the form of a hound.

Not a cute, cuddly basset hound with a penchant for wandering and a love of belly rubs. No, this creature could've been one of Artemis's hounds of the hunt, with sharp fangs that could tear a stag to pieces.

A glimmer of magic behind me caught my eye. I spun around. "Aiden, no!"

In a shimmer of amber and moss green magic, Aiden shifted into his fox form. His small body hunkered low to the ground, his lips a fierce snarl.

All I heard was blood roaring in my ears.

He was so much smaller than the creature. So vulnerable.

The words of a protection spell rose easily in me. I lent my energy in the unspoken spell, sending it out into the universe.

Artemis, goddess of wild things, protect him.

Brigid, goddess of the sacred flame, he and I are both of your fire. Watch over him.

Hecate, fierce lady of the crossroads, no place is your magic stronger than here. Keep him safe.

I imagined those three mighty goddesses guarding his small but strong form.

His eyes shone like determined embers on a night when the wind howled and the sky wept.

And me? I stood frozen, heart pounding, body swaying.

He glanced at me and yipped.

Run. It was Aiden's voice, a deep rumble, sounding in my head.

"No. I'm not leaving you."

The hound growled. The hairs on the back of my neck rose, and I *very* much wanted to run. But there was nowhere to run to. This was a realm of shadow, a place where magic slept, waiting to be born.

A place where magic slept…

That had to mean something, but my thoughts were sliding sideways like an out-of-control car on an icy, hilly road.

Aiden stood in front of me, a tiny fox guarding a witch of Willow Creek. Energy crackled in the air around us, a scent of ozone.

Maybe Aiden had a few tricks up his nonexistent sleeve? Something he could only access in his animal form? Crap. I knew so little about his shifter magic.

I knelt beside him, running my fingers through his fur. It wasn't as soft as I expected, but coarse, a little wiry. "Show me. I'll lend you my magic."

The shadow hound paced before us. Its eyes were the color of obsidian, their glint sharp and deadly.

I stood, holding my head high, hands balled fists at my sides, insides quivering. I wanted to say something befitting a warrior goddess, like Artemis herself.

"No," I said. "You will leave us alone."

Aiden glanced up at me. *I don't think that's going to work.*

"Do you have a better idea?" I said, my voice low, deliberate as I tried not to further provoke the magical beast about to eat us for dinner.

The shadow hound lowered its head. The creature was the size and shape of a huntress's gigantic wolfhound, except this one was made of pure magic. Its growl deepened.

Shit. It was preparing to attack.

Aiden's fox seemed to glow, shimmering with a barely contained mystical fire.

"I, too, am of the fire," I said. I held out my hands. My magic didn't exactly work that way. Even a fire witch couldn't summon actual fireballs. Much of our magic was unseen, an ability to connect with the world around us in powerful ways.

But this was the Crossroads of Magic, and though it was sick, it was still a powerful, sacred place. And if I was fae? Well, then who knew what I was capable of?

"We are the fire, the light, and the flame," I said, my voice deepening. I leaned into the place deep within from which my magic arose, the quiet place where it always waited.

"We are the fire, the light, and the flame," I repeated.

Nothing. If I expected something, some secret magic, to stir in me, I was hollowly disappointed. Only a quiet ache answered.

"We are the fire, the light, and the flame," I said again. My voice quivered as I spoke. I called again, and again.

Six times.

Seven times.

Eight.

Nine.

With a hunter's howl, the shadow hound lowered his head, pawing at the ground, preparing to attack.

But his target wasn't me.

It was Aiden.

CHAPTER NINE

Aiden

The creature reeked like death. The metallic tang of blood and the stink of rotting flesh singed my nose. Torn between an urge to run and a display of false bravado, I froze.

The hound, a being of shadow and evil magic brought suddenly to flesh-and-blood life, snarled at me, lowering its head.

Our eyes locked. Its eyes were hollow pits filled only with a memory of unseen darkness, like embers just as their light faded. Whatever being had created him was powerful and not to be trifled with.

And yet, we had trifled. All of us, the entire coven—or those who were left. And me, by waltzing in to rescue Evan. By even thinking of breaking the curse on my cousin, I had incurred a wrath I might not survive.

I'd be damned if I wouldn't go down fighting, fang and claw, fur and magic.

I wasn't a normal fox, after all. I was a shifter with a few tricks I generally preferred to keep to myself.

The shadow-hound circled. I circled right back. It hunkered low against the earth, and I puffed myself up, desperate to appear larger than I was.

Time. I needed to buy time.

Vi, I need you to run.

"No!" Her voice was sharp, a fear that pierced me.

No. I had to focus. To lose focus could very well mean death. Not just mine. Hers too. My heart lurched.

I'll be fine. I swear. But this will be easier if you run.

"No." Her voice was deep this time, full of conviction.

Goddess, but I could love her. And I didn't dare examine that thought—not now.

The hound stopped circling, lowering its head, ears pinned to its skull.

My body quivered. Vaguely, I heard Vi behind me, chanting an unfamiliar incantation. I could almost feel the force of her magic, the way I could feel a storm building in the air or a recent lightning strike.

I yipped at the hound, a come-and-get-me sound.

He lunged.

The cavern, the hound, the bed of moss, all flickered before me.

When it reappeared a mere half-second later, I was behind the hound, and it stood where I had only an instant earlier.

Vi gasped. He eyes flitted to me, her hand flying to a crystal at her throat, a piece of wire-wrapped tiger's eye that hung just below her rose quartz.

Courage, I mind-whispered to her. *We are both children of the sacred flame and holy earth. And I've got some tricks up my sleeve, just as you do. Focus your magic.*

She shook her head, and from my new vantage point, I could see the self-doubt in her eyes.

You can.

And then there was no time. The hound spun its gargantuan head around and glowered at me, a shimmer of angry light flashing in its black eyes.

I vanished once more, reappearing on a nearby boulder of obsidian-like rock, the surface slick like impossibly hard glass against my paws. I yipped, taunting the beast. Anything to distract it from Vi. I didn't have the magic to defeat it, but I had the magic to distract it while she came up with something that could.

The hound ran at me, full gallop, the sound of those paws the size of a horse's hooves pounding like thunder against the earthen floor. They echoed in the cavern.

I vanished, reappearing directly behind the hound. I yipped and disappeared again, appearing this time behind a large speckled toadstool.

But the hound was losing interest in me—that, or it had figured out I wasn't the easy prey.

Crap.

Crap.

Crap.

He turned away from me.

Now, head down, ears back, he'd focused his attention on Vi.

A growl rose from my throat. But I'd pushed too far. Why go for the teleporting fox when the hound could go after the fire witch? Or maybe it sensed her rising magic.

But she wasn't paying attention to the hound. Her eyes were fixed on the cavern above, on the impossibly large crystalline points, the luminescent moss, the labyrinth of roots.

I wanted to tell her to look down, to run, to move, but I doubted she could outrun it. Even in my fox form, I couldn't outrun the bloody thing. And if I distracted her from whatever magic she was calling, I could damn us both to a painful demise.

No.

I had to act.

The next time I reappeared, I was on the shadow-hound's back. My teeth sunk into its smoky black fur.

Ash. It tasted like ash, and sulfur, and blood. It tasted like the evil magic that had given birth to it. A fury unlike any I'd ever known flowed through me as my teeth dug into that fur, seeking the flesh beneath—and finding none.

Because it had none?

The creature howled, more a howl of frustration and anger than pain. Certainly not pain.

It shook itself.

Sharp teeth caught hold of my tail. I squealed in pain like a kit.

The shadow-hound tossed me like a frisbee across the cavern.

My vision wavered, spots dancing across the world, but I refused to release my hold on consciousness. Staggering, I rose.

A warrior's cry filled the cavern. Vi.

A blinding fork of light crackled from the ceiling to the hound.

The shadow-hound didn't whimper. Instead, there was a horrendous sound, like a specter's sickening groan in a haunted castle, as the mystically charged lightning hit the beast.

I sank to the ground, panting.

When my eyes recovered from the flash of light, only a charred spot on the ground remained where the shadow-hound had stood.

And then Vi was sweeping me into her arms, planting a thousand kisses in my fur, a state that, despite my bruises, I didn't exactly mind.

Vi

My lips brushed his fur. I buried my face in that rough, coppery hair, so full of wildness and magic. And a little cunning, perhaps.

"Goddess damn it, Aiden McPherson. Don't do crazy shit like that!"

A guy could get used to this.

"Ugh. Don't make jokes. You almost died. And I had the situation under control." I sat down on the packed earth and settled him in my lap. "Are you hurt? Bleeding?"

I ran my hands gingerly over his small body. He was far longer than Rosemary Caterwaul Broomsticks, but didn't weigh much more, a fact that I found rather terrifying. In his fox form, Aiden seemed so small, so vulnerable.

When I got to Aiden's tail, he jumped away.

No. The single word was almost a growl.

"You're hurt. Let me see."

It will heal.

He turned away from me and disappeared behind a boulder. He wasn't moving as agilely as he had been before he'd been tossed by the shadow-hound.

"Aiden, will you come back if I promise not to touch your tail?"

A deep, warm chuckle was his only response. He popped his head over the top of the bounder. "You're free to touch my tail, such as it is now."

"Not the time," I said, but I couldn't fight the racing of my heart. And now, it wasn't racing out of fear. Nope. Definitely not fear.

He waggled his eyebrows. "Surprised? If you're going to shift, you've got to strip."

"Nice. Did you make that up yourself?"

He shook his head. "Nope. Old shifter saying."

"I have a lot to learn."

"It seems to me you learn quickly. Or did you master the art of summoning lightning long ago?"

I frowned. The act had drained me, and I didn't want to admit that my head ached from that burst of magic. "No. It's new."

Our eyes locked. So much was unsaid—so much we needed to say.

I swallowed, hard. I needed a thousand cups of tea and an entire cookie jar of Cassie's homemade gingersnaps before I felt up to having difficult conversations. "You know, there might be more of those things around here. We should probably get moving."

He nodded. "Slight problem. I seem to have, uh, lost my clothes in the shift."

"Oh." I swallowed again, from a completely different emotion. This one far less unpleasant. "Right."

"I have an idea," he said. "But I don't know if you'll like it."

"Try me." Heat throbbed at the apex of my legs.

"This place, magical though it may be, is not the astral. And though it holds the key to rescuing Evan and stopping whatever dark force is out to steal the magic of the Crossroads—and Willow Creek—for itself...I don't think we have what we need. Not yet. But there's someplace that might have it."

I folded my arms over my chest, fighting off a tangle of emotions. "What exactly do we need? A weapon?"

"The greatest weapon of all time."

"Care to clue me in?"

Aiden grinned, so much the fox, even in his delicious human form. "Knowledge."

I snorted. "So, we go to the astral again…and do what?"

He stepped around the boulder. I sucked in a breath, a sound I knew he heard. Sweet Goddess. Could Aphrodite herself have dreamt up such a pleasing form? He quickly closed the space between us and grasped my hand. I could tell by the state of him that he felt the same desire I did, but he didn't act on it.

"We ask for guidance."

"Aiden…if the being who created that place is fae? Well, they're not famous for their helpfulness."

"I think, for you, they might make an exception."

I glanced around. The air was still and stunk of lingering sulfur and ash. Another shadow-hound could come along, and I didn't have another magical lightning bolt in me.

And as much as the truth, whatever it might be, scared me? Well, I needed it.

And somehow, I was ready. With Aiden by my side, I was ready.

I pressed my lips to his. His mouth opened willingly, a deep moan that matched my own. Was this what kissing was supposed to feel like? Molten, like liquid fire rising up from my very soul?

Because, if so, count me in.

I groaned through the pleasure of his kiss, drawing our bodies closer together.

I tried to tell myself it was just desire.

But its roots were deep inside of me, in a place that went far beyond lust and passion.

The crystal in my pocket seemed to grow heavier, heavier. Not the hag stone, but the purple ametrine. Two stones, combined. Citrine: the dream made manifest. Amethyst: spirit awoken.

Aiden slid his fingers through my hair. I leaned into his touch, lost in the pleasure of it.

"Vi." Aiden's whisper was almost pained. "Vi, look."

I reluctantly withdrew from the ecstatic spell of our kiss.

A fine mist of rain fell against our skin. The waterfall cascaded once more into its crystalline pool, and the tall, wide trees with their twisting branches drank in the rain. The place in the astral. Somehow, we'd made it.

"She returns."

I spun around to find a woman who instantly reminded me of the Empress from the tarot. A pair of hunter green breeches hugged her legs, along with a pair of brown leather boots that came to mid-ankle. She wore a pair of dark green bracers and a matching leather corset, both laced with black cord, and a ruffled ivory top underneath.

No. I saw now she wasn't the Empress, but the High Priestess, one who lived in service to magic and spirit. I bowed slightly.

"My lady."

She sniggered and waved her hand. "No need for such formalities—especially not when your companion is skyclad."

I cleared my throat, fingering the tiger's eye I'd donned earlier. Courage. Strength. And I needed both in droves at the moment. "My...we've come to ask..." I trailed off. Come to ask what? The awkward introvert in me wished I'd planned this better.

She shook her head. "I know. I've been waiting for twenty-one years. Normally, for me, such a span of time is a mere season, but this time, it felt so long." She eyed Aiden, amusement in her gaze. "Will this do for now?"

I glanced at him. He was now clad in a pair of black linen trousers and a moss-green tunic. Simple, minimalist, a bit dated, but the look definitely suited him.

He inclined his head. "Nicely."

"First, you'll rest, and then we'll talk." She turned and began to lead us toward a wide, fern-lined path in the forest, gesturing that we should follow.

"Wait," Aiden said, seizing my arm as I started to follow, rather dumbstruck. "Time passes differently here. And we're kind of in the middle of a time-sensitive situation."

She nodded. "You know your lore, fox-kin. But don't worry. This place isn't within the boundaries of the faerie realm. This place is the astral, and time doesn't actually pass here at all. Does that ease your worries?"

His grip on my arm relaxed. "It does."

"Then follow me."

The wide path, bordered on each side by ferns, bluebells, and other assorted wildflowers, wended through the forest. The mist of rain was cool, but not cold, a gentle balm against my skin.

I felt jittery inside, a feeling that wasn't quite anxious, but far from peaceful. Perhaps, it was merely the aftereffects of my adrenaline-fueled magic?

The magic of this world, some small pocket of the astral realm, felt pure and fresh. Neither good nor evil, it seemed to exist outside the realms of humankind. This was the sort of magic that simply *was*, something wild and sacred.

We stopped at a hedge of vines. They looked familiar. My tattoo. I'd thought the vine, with its thorns and flowers, was some remnant of a dream my artist friend made tangible. Yet here it was—that same vine, with its distinctive purple flowers.

I couldn't help studying her, this captivating fae stranger. Her very presence was magnetic. Was she a warrior or a priestess? Was she both? I knew her at once to be fae, but I didn't know whether the fae realm held such clear delineations as the human.

She raised a hand, bidding us to pause. She bowed her head and held her arms at her sides, palms facing the tall, thick hedge.

"Gnomes of earth who protect this space, open now the secret gate."

With a shimmer of green light, an opening appeared in the hedge.

We stepped through to a teeming cottage garden, filled with stone benches and flagstone pathways. A small creek meandered its way through a hodgepodge of plants, ranging from woody rosemary to large pink roses, from yarrow to foxglove.

And in the center of it all sat a stone cottage. Tiny faeries fluttered on gossamer wings. The air smelled like rain and sunshine, like flowers and herbs and moss, the best of a wild forest and a sunny meadow.

I sucked in a breath, in awe of it all.

"Is this real?" I asked. My cheeks immediately reddened. I shook my head. "I'm sorry. Of course it's not real."

The fae woman frowned. She held out her hand, and a small faerie alighted on her inner wrist. The creature was a mere six inches tall, their face a mossy green, with a shimmer of bronze overtop. The being's eyes were blue like sapphires, and those iridescent wings never stopped moving.

The woman chuckled as the tiny faerie eyed me curiously. "It's all right, Thorne. They're friends. Witch and fox and human and a little bit of fae too. But friends."

With a chirping sound, Thorne nodded and flew away.

The fae woman turned her attention back to us. "This place is real. It is a sanctuary. For fae. For elementals. For any magical creature in need of refuge."

I was going to guess that included us at this particular moment.

I turned to Aiden, unsure how to proceed. Despite his cleverness, he, too, seemed a bit at a loss for words.

She smiled. "Vivienne, you of all beings know what a comfort a good cup of tea can be in times of distress. I offer you sanctuary, a full teapot, and a warm bed. When the sun rises here, no time will have passed in your world, but your strength will be renewed."

I sucked in a breath, not daring to ask, but knowing I needed to say we hadn't come here for the bed-and-breakfast experience.

Before I could summon the courage to speak, Aiden did. "That's very kind, but we've come seeking something else."

She approached the door of the cottage. Like her garb, it was deep green, though the round, stained glass window set in it was a swirl of deep purple, vivid teal, and pumpkin orange. "Rest. I think you will find all that you seek and more within these walls."

She bowed her head and gestured toward the closed door. "I'll see you when the enchanted sun rises. Blessed be, fox and witch. Blessed be."

And then she walked through the hedge—as if it wasn't even there—leaving Aiden and I standing in a wild cottage garden surrounded by tiny faeries whose wings hummed like the summery buzz of dragonflies.

CHAPTER TEN

Aiden

I cleared my throat, a bit stunned, to say the least, but also fighting a growing exhaustion. Shifter magic was meant to be used sparingly, and I'd used up more than my share of it. No shifting for me anytime soon, that was for sure.

I stepped forward, along the flagstone path lined with low-growing thyme and bushes of spiky lavender. I inhaled deeply, scents of everything from moss to lavender to spearmint sweeping over me. I'd spent six weeks in the mountains of New Hampshire, tending a faerie witch's garden, but damn, the magic in this place was stronger and wilder yet.

At the front door, I turned back to Vi. She was worrying her lower lip, clearly uncertain.

"Shall we?" I asked.

She shrugged, but I sensed her trepidation. "Sure. Why not?"

"We asked for answers. And it sounds like they're behind this door." I pushed the door open. It gave way with a soft, sleepy creak.

I stepped inside, unable to help myself. "Whoa. Are you seeing this?" If books and magical knickknacks could make a guy salivate like a medium-rare filet mignon, this place would do it. Inside the cottage was a magical scholar's paradise.

The floors were flagstone covered with soft rugs in rusty red. The shelves were weathered wood lined with leather-bound volumes, all somehow shining in jewel tones. Four chairs with velvet cushions flanked a round pedestal table. One chair was cushioned in crimson red, another in turquoise blue, another in sage green, and the last in sapphire-hued fabric. I recognized the colors as representing the four elements—fire, air, earth, and water.

The shelves weren't just home to magical tomes. There were rows of crystals, from tall pointed towers to polished spheres, from glass jars of tumbled stones to smaller points and larger clusters. Chalices, daggers, rows of amulets and talismans hanging from a tree-shaped stand...anything a witch could ask for.

"Sweet Brigid," Vi gasped, her trepidation seeming to vanish. "It's like a new-age shop on steroids."

"I suspect these aren't just baubles. There's magical energy in this room. Sleeping, but waiting to be awoken." The magic shimmered over me, speaking of moonlight and mysteries. "Each object has a story to tell—and not just the books."

Vi's hands covered her face, but I could sense her excitement. She was giddy. The flush I glimpsed in her cheeks as she withdrew her hands to study an amethyst sphere was from joy.

"I'd like to live in a place just like this someday," she said. "A lovely garden to grow ingredients for my tea blends—and a place for Rosemary Caterwaul Broomsticks to sun and watch the world go by. And this." She spread her arms wide, gesturing to the cottage's interior, and beamed at me, and I couldn't help beaming right back. I crossed the room to where she stood, staring at the amethyst sphere.

"We can have it someday, Vi. You and me."

She straightened, frowning at me. "Yeah…"

Did I dare tell her what my fox knew—what my fox had known from the moment I'd met her? "Foxes mate for life." I cringed. "That. I'm sorry. Crap." I spun to face the window. "I don't mean if I sleep with someone, I'm mystically betrothed to them. It's more complicated like that, an ancient shifter handfasting ritual with magic and spells and…" I stopped talking, keenly aware I was babbling like a fool.

Silence fell—the awkward kind.

She was the first one to speak. "It's just like…like we've known each other for a long time." Her words were soft, but not afraid.

I turned to her, nodding. "Like every step on our journeys didn't just lead us to Willow Creek."

"Exactly." Vi's stomach growled, interrupting our conversation. "I need food. That magic took it out of me."

"Me too."

There was a pot of beef stew hanging above a low fire. I poured us each a bowlful while Vi poured tea into the waiting mugs on the table.

We plopped into a couple chairs and dug in, each devouring two bowls of the hearty stew and hunks of soda bread. The tea was spearmint with something else.

"Lavender," Vi said, savoring a cup of tea after her second bowl of stew. "Lavender, spearmint, and lemon balm. You wouldn't think those would work together, but it's perfect."

"Mmm," I agreed.

I added a few logs onto the fire to keep it going. The light outside was growing dimmer, evening shadows sliding over us, though I wasn't quite sure how that worked in the astral realm. Some sort of enchantment, perhaps?

I lit a couple of black tallow candles that were on the rough-hewn mantle above the fireplace, carrying them over to the table, careful not to drip any wax on our faerie hostess's rug.

"Where do we even begin?" I said, eyeing the hundreds of books and endless magical items that lined the shelves.

"I wish Cassie were here," Vi said with a sigh, setting her mug on the table and rising to stretch. "She has this way of knowing."

"In some of the old texts, it's called the Kenning. Some have it from birth. Others are blessed with it after an encounter with the fae."

"I don't think Cassie had any encounters with the fae."

"No. But she's met the Guardian. And the Guardian is fae-blessed."

"So, why are we here and not her?" Vi asked.

"That's what we're here to find out."

She sent me a pointed glare. "That's not a helpful answer."

I chuckled. I couldn't help but enjoy a bit of friendly verbal sparring with Vi.

I rose. I was bruised, and the more tired I grew, the more I knew I'd be really sore in the morning. And maybe my poor tail would always be a little crooked.

"Do you still have the hag stone?"

She nodded and fished it out of her pocket. "Right here. Why?"

"This cottage and its garden are teeming with faerie magic. If anything could lead us to the right item, it would be the stone."

"Last time I looked through it, we fell into the Crossroads."

"Last time you looked through it, we were looking for Evan. And that's the last place that Evan was…himself."

"So, you're saying, if I focus on seeking something that can help us end the curse, the hag stone can guide me?"

"Worth a shot."

She worried the stone in her palm. "If I start to disappear, you grab my hand. Promise me."

I brushed a quick kiss against her cheek. "I promise. But it won't come to that." I kissed her other cheek, letting my lips travel to her earlobe. "I believe in you, Vivienne. In your heart. In your strength. In your magic."

I could feel the moment her pulse quickened. "Is that the man speaking? Or the fox?"

I kissed her jaw. "Both."

Vi

Aiden McPherson may have been the most sinfully distracting man I'd ever met. He sent me spinning. Deep conversations yielded to powerful emotions; innocent touches led to quickening desires...all of it laced with a magic I wasn't quite sure I understood.

I'd found belonging over the years. First in Savannah, with my friend Ivy and the Mystic Magnolias Coven her mother and grandmother co-led. Then in Willow Creek, with Bailee and Cassie and Nick.

But what Aiden offered wasn't mere companionship. It was, well, a partner. A mate. I wasn't sure I believed in soulmates, but if anyone could make me believe, it was this quick-witted, soft-spoken fox with his secret humor and hidden wisdom.

I squeezed my hand around the plain white stone, then unfurled my fingers like a midnight blossom opening to the moon's silver light. Outside, the daylight yielded to night. An owl's hoot carried.

I closed my eyes, grounding my energy. As a fire witch, I struggled to stay grounded, and imagining myself as a tree with roots stretching deep into the earth helped me keep my energy from going all...well, wonky.

When I opened my eyes, I felt calmer. My body swayed, and Aiden guided me into a chair with a crimson cushion, positioning it so I could easily turn to see most of the contents of the shelves.

I raised the stone up toward my eye. Often, I called on Brigid, a Celtic fire goddess, but her energy didn't seem right for this work. "Cerridwen," I whispered. "She who stirs a sacred cauldron, crone of wisdom and keeper of secrets, guide my vision."

I raised the stone to my eye and blinked. "Guide my vision," I repeated. "Guide me."

When I peered through the stone, the room seemed different. I'd never thought objects could have auras, but these seemed to. Wisps of magical energy trailed along the spines of books, from fiery orange to aquamarine and sage's pale green. From crystal to amulet, dagger to chalice, from one book to the next, I looked.

After what seemed like hours of this, I let the hand holding the stone drop, sighing in frustration. "Nothing. Everything looks different when viewed through the stone, but nothing looks different enough to tell me it's why we're here."

I rolled my wrists, trying to get some movement back into my body. Feeling edgy, I stood and went to the window. Night had fallen, and through the clear glass, the garden shone with luminescent splendor.

Aiden joined me, putting a hand around my waist and drawing me close. "It was worth a try. We just have to keep looking." He kissed the top of my head. "It's beautiful here, isn't it?"

I nodded, leaning against him. I almost wished we could stay here, in a place where time didn't move, where the rising and setting of the sun and the wheeling of the stars in the sky were some mere trickery of magic and not indications of the passing of time.

"She said she'd be back at dawn."

"We have time, then. The sun just set."

"How long was I looking through the stone?"

"About forty-five minutes would be my guess. I took a look around this place. The stairs lead to a bedroom underneath a glass ceiling, and I've never seen stars so bright. And a clawfoot tub that seems mystically full of hot water."

I wrinkled my nose. "You're making this up."

He grinned slyly. "Am I?" He headed to the stairs, holding out his hand. "You're exhausted. I'm exhausted. And I think that, despite the astral, I've developed a bit of an odor."

I approached him and gave him a playful sniff. "A bit." I laughed. "Fine. Show me this fairytale oasis you describe."

We climbed up the wide wooden stairs. I didn't remember the house having a second story, but sure enough, there it was.

"You weren't kidding." Before me was maybe—just maybe—the most beautiful, romantic, fairytale-inspired room I'd ever seen. The ceiling was glass, revealing a smattering of impossibly bright stars glittering like colorful fairy lights in an inky sky. The wooden headboard of the bed was painted emerald green and had a scene of deep blue mountains that reminded me of Willow Creek, set amid the Blue Ridge Mountains of Virginia. The bedspread was a patchwork quilt in jewel tones, the sheets plum-hued and satiny.

And, sure enough, a steaming clawfoot tub stood in one corner. The water was clear and promised to soothe weary muscles. A wooden shelf decorated with moss and crystals held various jars of bath salts.

"It's like a dream come true."

Aiden leaned against the oaken banister at the top of the stairs, his expression thoughtful. "I think maybe...I don't know...we made it."

"We did? Not the fae woman?"

"It wasn't here before. I think somehow, we needed this. A brief respite before we plunge back into the fray."

I nodded, my stomach tightening. "It's coming, isn't it? This terrible battle between evil and good? Whatever is out there, trying to take over the Crossroads, kill the Guardian, destroy Willow Creek and the coven...it's getting closer."

Aiden approached me, taking my hand and drawing it to his mouth. He brushed a featherlight kiss across my knuckles, and I shivered, though the room was warm. "It is. We're strong enough to face it. The gathering storm, whatever form it takes."

I had my doubts. But the quiet faith in his voice, the determination and warmth in his gaze when it locked with mine?

Those were almost enough to make me believe.

"I've been running for two years," he said. "Chasing something elusive. Peace? Answers? Who knows what? And Willow Creek is my peace, my answer. You, Vivienne Gearhart. You are my peace, my answer. The fox knew before the man did. It always does."

I nodded. "I'm so used to being cautious, afraid, planning for every dangerous eventuality. But with you, the danger isn't in acting. It's in letting the moments we're together slip away."

His fingers entwined in mine. A jolt of desire shot through me, and he stepped closer. "We've been given a gift. This place. A sliver of peace in a world of chaos, a waking dream. Let's enjoy it."

His lips met mine, and my moan as his mouth plundered mine was instantaneous. And intense. When he drew away, I strained toward him, not wanting it to end.

He smiled, a smile that promised ecstasy in his touch. And I *needed* it.

He approached the wooden shelf and plucked a jar from between the crystal points. He unscrewed the lid, examining the contents and holding it out so I could take a sniff.

I smiled. "Rose petals, lavender oil. And a touch of sandalwood and vanilla." A combination of scents that promised sensual pleasures.

He held it over the waiting tub of steaming water, tilting it ever-so-slightly. "Shall I?"

"Yes."

He added a large quantity of the salts. Rose petals floated to the surface of the water. He swirled his fingers in the tub to help the salts dissolve.

He replaced the jar on the stand. My body was full-on trembling now.

He kissed my cheek, my jaw. "You're shaking."

"Not in a bad way," I assured him.

I tugged at the bottom of his tunic, easing it over his head and letting it drop to the floor. One by one, clothes landed on hardwood. He took my hand and guided me into the tub. It was more than large enough for both of us to fit comfortably, and he clamored in. We sat cross-legged, facing each other in the hot water.

His gaze took in every inch of me, leaving trails of heat everywhere.

"Vi, love," he murmured low and husky as he knelt to capture first one breast, then the other in his mouth. "You have such beautiful freckles everywhere."

I tilted my head back, clasping his shoulders. There were no words for what he was doing to me. I reached for his erection, hand skimming his thigh. When my fingers grasped its thick, hard length, he moaned.

"We should take our time," he said, though his words of protest were weak.

"Next time. Not now. Now I need you."

I climbed on top of him. I'd never been so bold, always too self-conscious, but with Aiden, I had no desire to not express exactly what I wanted, to hold back from going for it.

I guided his length inside of me, both of us crying out as he penetrated me.

I began to move, a slow rocking that quickly gave way to a frenzied rhythm. He reached between us, his thumb expertly fingering my clit as I rode him.

That act undid me. I came once, twice, a third time. My eyes rolled back in my head, heart pounding. A kaleidoscope of colors danced before my vision as he sent me tumbling, again and again.

In a deep, throaty cry, Aiden came, his orgasm joining my own.

I was spent, thoroughly and completely, and sated. Still inside of me, he rose and moved us both to the bed, laying me down on the velvety quilt. I gazed up at him, my fox with his dark hair and amber eyes, framed now by starlight.

I touched his face, drawing him in for a kiss.

"I didn't know that was possible," I said, my tongue heavy.

"I think we've only grazed the surface of what's possible," he said, voice rough and breathy.

I don't remember climbing under the covers, or the sleep that claimed me. Only waking again and again, bringing each other to pleasure a few more times throughout the night.

CHAPTER ELEVEN

Aiden

It was dark when I awoke. Stars still gleamed above in the sky, but their light wasn't quite as sharp. The sky held the promise of coming sunrise.

Beside me, Vi slept, waves of deep red hair framing her pale skin—from her face with its button nose, to the curve of her shoulders, to the gentle rise and fall of her breasts.

It felt right. Like our bodies had known how to pleasure the other, a lost memory from a previous lifetime brought to the surface by our meeting in this one.

I recalled that night on my parents' estate, and the bitter taste of the potion they'd forced down my throat. The memory of my family's betrayal stung worse than the potion itself, the way my fox had cowered and cringed.

But beyond the pain of severed ties was a memory of intoxicating magic. That magic? It had been Vi. Of that I was sure. This moment, this night spent in the astral, was the culmination of a journey that started with an indescribable magic that called to me.

I slipped out of bed and dressed quietly, making my way downstairs.

As soon as I reached the bottom step, my gaze swept around the room. The fire still crackled in the fireplace, but the rest of the room looked undisturbed.

Except for the figure who leaned against one of the bookcases.

Startled, I felt the shift begin to take over, but the fae woman—the same one from the night before—approached quickly and placed her hand on my shoulder.

"No. Not now."

The magic of the shift faded at her touch, which felt cool, like a mountain stream rushing over sunburnt skin.

I studied her, fox and man taking her in.

"Who are you?"

Her lips, like dark rubies, curled in a winsome smile. "Kin."

"Not mine." It wasn't a question.

She shook her head, a quick half shake.

I glanced up the stairs but heard no sounds to indicate Vi had awakened. I had a lot of questions. I didn't know where to start. Some of them weren't mine to ask.

But I had one that was. "Why am I here? How can I help my cousin?"

"The witch you call Evan."

"Yes."

The fae woman gestured toward the table. "Sit."

I knew that the fae weren't always trustworthy, but I trusted her. She was a caretaker to the beings here, to a place of pure magic, a mystical sanctuary out of space and time. That was not the work of a malevolent being.

I sat in a chair with a deep green cushion. The fae woman pushed open the window. Cool breeze, scented with mossy forest, fragrant flowers, and earthy herbs, swept through the room. It tangled with the scents of woodsmoke, candlewax, and dried herbs, all of it promising magic.

The woman poured us each a cup of tea. I wrapped my hands around the sage green mug, a spiral painted in black on its side. I knew the fae woman had a name—one I had an inkling I already knew.

"She is fire and grace—sweet, sacred magic," the fae woman said, stirring honey into her tea and then sliding the jar across the table.

I nodded and sipped. The blend was fruity with a hint of something floral—like blackberries and apples mixed with rosehips.

"You like it."

"The tea? Yes." The whole beating-around-the-bush thing? Not so much.

"I made it for her. For today."

"What is today?" I asked.

"A reunion." It wasn't the fae woman who answered. It was Vi. She stood at the foot of the stairs, her hair unrestrained and a tad wild. She'd traded her human clothes for a garb similar to the ones the fae woman had worn yesterday. They looked tailor-made for her—and not just the size.

A deep purple shirt with flowing sleeves was topped by a black leather corset. Her pants were black, not wool or linen but something in between. She wore her rose quartz necklace again, but an aura quartz point set in silver filigree hung on a slightly longer chain below it.

Without realizing I was doing so, I rose. "Vi."

I felt suddenly stiff, awkward.

She smiled, crossing the room to kiss my cheeks. She squeezed my hands. "I know, Aiden."

"Care to clue me in?"

"Gladly."

Vi

I poured myself a cup of tea. Normally, my hands would be shaking as my head whirled with so much new and overwhelming information. But I didn't feel anxious. I felt...at peace. A piece of me had been missing. Or maybe, a few pieces.

I started to sit at the table, but I was too keyed up, so I stood and gazed out the window, where a new day dawned. The forest was still filled with shadows, but birds sang in the trees, and a few of the tiny faeries with their iridescent wings flitted through the garden. Pixies, I now recognized.

How could a single night of lovemaking and dreaming change everything? How could I awaken to know so much more than I had mere hours before?

"What's wrong?" Aiden asked, and I didn't have to turn to him to see his frown. I *heard* it.

I spun to face him, a smile tugging at my lips. "You were right. I'm a faerie. Well, part faerie. Part fae? Which is it?"

"Either will do, sweet Vivienne." The other woman stood. How had I not seen it, the resemblance? Our height, cheekbones, the color of our hair. She smiled, the crow's feet around her eyes the only sign of her age. "Granddaughter."

She didn't take me in her arms in some sort of melodramatic embrace. Her hands clasped both of mine, stacked on top of each other, and the affection in her eyes said all I needed to know. I knew why she hadn't come for me, that she couldn't leave this place without others learning of the sanctuary she kept here. And I knew why she'd come here in the first place.

Aiden cleared his throat.

I forced myself to sit down at the table. "It came to me in a dream, swift, in an instant, like a movie of long-lost memories playing at double speed. I am part fae. And not just any fae. I'm a descendent of the fae sisters who sent the Guardian to protect the Crossroads."

Aiden's gaze was dark, serious, yet decidedly analytical. "That's why you were drawn to Willow Creek."

"For those of us who are meant to be there, all roads lead there," I said, repeating the line as it came to me, in crystal clarity, upon waking.

"You're talking in faerie riddles already," he chided.

I winced. "Sorry."

"I need more details."

My grandmother chuckled. I glanced at her. "What do I call you, anyway? Grandma?"

She refilled her mug and Aiden's. "Call me Nene."

"Nene." I tested the name out on my lips and tongue, committing it to memory.

"My father was one of Nene's sons—half-human, half-fae."

"Was?" Aiden asked, glancing at Nene.

She shook her head, her expression pained. "He's not with us anymore. I was blessed with twin sons, Iain and Weylin. Iain was like an owl, filled with moonlight and able to travel easily between the worlds, a conduit for wisdom and magic in any of them. Weylin...he never found his path. And the more he tried, the more he became convinced that the spell my sister and I cast to give the Guardian her gifts, to protect the Crossroads and the magic of Willow Creek, was the reason. Foolishness, of course.

"The truth was Weylin had a warrior's blood, but he wanted that of a mage, like his brother. He killed Iain twenty-two years ago. Not long after, a baby girl was born, with fae magic singing sweetly in her aura. I visited her, held her in my arms that autumn day in Georgia, and stole the secrets of the fae away from her so that he couldn't trace them with a spell. I brought them here, that she should sleep and that, upon waking, they would be returned. But I feared if I ever left this place, Weylin would find those memories—and find her."

As she spoke, Aiden's features grew alarmed, his fists clasping, skin reddening. "Weylin? This Weylin...is it Weylin Felson?"

"That was his father's surname, yes."

I glanced between them. This—whatever this was—had not been in my dream-vision. "Felson? As in, Nick and Evan Felson?"

"Their father? Nick and Evan's father is fae?" I couldn't picture Nick Felson as part fae, no matter how hard I tried.

Nene answered. "He is. I didn't know what Weylin had planned until he attacked the Guardian. That deceit, his pursuit of Maeve, the birth of his sons, he covered well." She pursed her lips in a dark, unreadable frown. "I made a mistake with Weylin. I thought if I gave him time, he'd find a place of acceptance. I can't undo the damage that mistake has done. But I can help you save Evan, the Crossroads of Magic, and Willow Creek."

I sipped my tea. The taste was pleasant, somehow blending each of the four elements into one perfect beverage. But even that blending of earth, air, water, and fire, the mingling of fruity and earthy notes on my tongue, couldn't dislodge the knot that formed in my gut.

I'd never known my grandmother. She'd dropped my mom off on Granddad's doorstep. And though Granddad had his share of problems, at least he'd manned up and cared for his daughter — and later, after my mom passed, for his granddaughter.

Nene speared me with her gaze. Her smile was sad.

"I know, faerie child."

My lips faltered in a failed smile. "Know what?"

"He loved you. Your grandfather. He was with your mother that day, and I handed you to him. I saw in your mother's eyes that she wouldn't last long. It wasn't in my power to save her. I saw that you would have your trials. My heart broke a thousand times, knowing I couldn't stop them. In order to save your life, I had to leave you in his care. And he did care."

I would *not* cry. "I know." I sniffed.

Aiden's hand sought mine. I wanted to lean into him, though I wasn't the type to lean into anyone.

"Vivienne Rose Gearhart, the magic that sings in you is witch and faerie. You are born of summer and autumn, of fire and earth. You will do great things. And you have always been loved. I saw it in your mother's eyes, and in your grandfather's. And this morning..." She glanced between me and Aiden, and I blushed. Nothing like meeting your long-lost faerie grandmother and her totally knowing you had mind-blowing sex in her cottage the night before. Not awkward at all.

Another thought occurred to me, and I set my now-empty mug down with a thud on the table.

"Are you saying that Nick and Evan are, what, my cousins?"

She wrapped her long fingers around her mug. There was dirt under her nails, which were just a little too long. I sensed earthy magic in her aura, a calm, stable strength with deep roots. Wisdom and thoughtfulness. "I am. Are you ready to meet Evan? Well, part of Evan."

"I've met Evan."

Aiden cleared his throat. I turned to him, to his amber gaze, flecked this morning with deep, rusty brown. Nene leaned forward, resting her chin in her palm. He glanced between us, as if suddenly a bit nervous under my grandmother's intense gaze but proceeded. "I think I know what your grandmother is getting at."

Her lips curled into a grin almost as sly as Aiden's so often was. "You are every bit as clever as your aura suggests, little fox."

She continued. "The magic that made Nettie Woodruff the Guardian of the Crossroads of Magic beneath Willow Creek changed her very nature. It made her stronger. It made her immortal. It gave her a deep knowing and connection to natural magicks, though such things are normally reserved for the fae. When my sister and I cast the spell, we didn't just bestow her with faerie gifts. We gave her pieces of ourselves.

"So, when Weylin decided to reclaim the Crossroads, he soon learned that he couldn't just waltz in and take it. And the Guardian's magic has a life of its own. He couldn't steal it. He couldn't merely cast a spell to defeat her." A pained expression flickered across her face. Her skin paled, long lashes fluttering down as she closed her eyes, as if remembering.

"But blood magic is powerful. Weylin might not have his brother's gifts and wisdom, but he has cunning. He has that in spades. And he knew that part of his mother and aunt's magic sang in Nettie's immortal body. He thought that would be enough to break her ties to the Crossroads. It wasn't."

No. My hand flew to my stomach—because I knew where this was heading.

Nene pressed forward with her story. "But the Guardian was a flesh-and-blood woman once. A witch, a wise woman, yet a woman. And so he married one of her kin—a granddaughter of a granddaughter of her sister— and he waited. In Evan's dreams, Weylin convinced him to cast that spell one year ago. It gave Weylin power over Nettie. Evan and Nick, Ginny and Maeve are all mortal."

I stood up, my chair scraping the hardwood floor. Blood roared in my ears.

"They're in danger."

Nene nodded. "Very much so. Alive, but in danger. On the black moon, he'll cast the spell."

"The black moon, what is that?"

It was Aiden who spoke. "You know how the blue moon is the second full moon in a given calendar month?"

I nodded.

He continued, his voice flat and grim. "The black moon is the second new moon in a calendar month."

My hand flew to my neck, my thumb rubbing the crystal at my throat. "That's soon, isn't it?" I sucked in a few shallow breaths. "Tell us how. Tell us what to do, how to stop him."

"Sit," Nene instructed. She rose and fetched a small blue vial, dabbing some of it onto a bit of brown cloth.

I sat, and she rubbed the cloth against my temples. I breathed in, a few deep, grounding breaths. The scents, blends of hyssop, chamomile, and lavender, calmed me— but only a little. Enough that I could listen. I'd been alone and adrift for a long time. Willow Creek and our tiny coven were my home, my family. I couldn't lose it.

"One step at a time," she said softly. She set the vial on the table. "The rest of my tale is far from pretty, but I need to tell it."

I nodded. She was right.

"Weylin underestimated the Guardian's strength, her resourcefulness. She had plans in motion. For one, Cassandra—your great-aunt. The Guardian couldn't send Cassandra forward in time. To do so would violate the laws of magic. But she could tether the young witch's spirit to something that would hold her in stasis until the proper time. Fittingly, she chose an oak tree." A slight smile curled Nene's lips. "That spell had an added benefit. It gave Cassandra and Nicholas an opportunity to meet in this lifetime at the right time, so that their love wouldn't go unrequited until the next time they were reborn."

"Is that why Cassie is so powerful?"

Nene nodded. "Yes. An odd side effect of the Guardian's spell. So much time in silence, roots deep in the earth, roots deep in magic. Cassie has the knowing. She always will—in this life, and in all others."

Wow. I'd have to store that tidbit to tell Cassie later. It explained a lot.

"And Evan?"

"Yes. When the time comes, on the black moon, you and the coven will face Weylin. I don't know—none of us does—what the outcome will be. But at this moment, you have a more important task. To end the curse that Weylin set loose on Evan."

"Why? Evan did what Weylin wanted. He cast the spell. Why curse him?" Aiden asked.

"Because he's a sicko?" I offered.

"The truth is more complicated. Evan challenged Weylin. When he realized he'd been used, that his entire coven was trapped on another plane of existence, he fought back. Weylin cursed him. I suspect he meant to kill him, but, gratefully, they were on the astral at the time. The curse separated Evan's true nature, his deep self, from his physical body. His physical self is suffering, separated from the truest essence of his spirit."

She locked eyes with me. "Evan is your cousin, Vi. Your kin. Take him home. Together with the family you've discovered, help him heal. It will take time."

I nodded. "Of course."

Aiden stood. He knelt before my grandmother. With his black hair and amber eyes, in his tunic and britches, he looked for all the world like a knight pledging his fealty to a queen. And my grandmother? She seemed equal parts amused and pleased.

"Take us to him. Please. Take us to him and tell us how to help him."

She patted his shoulder. "You are a fierce and loyal companion, worthy of my granddaughter. There's a path, beyond the hedgerow, that will lead you to him. Follow the song. He's like a bird, that one. Always singing. The love and strength of your coven will help him."

She frowned, rising abruptly and beginning to pace. When she turned to me, her eyes were dark with worry. "I can't go with you. I've remained so long in this place that the transition back to my earthly body will take years—and my body remains in the realm of the fae, where my sister tends to me. It might be years before we see each other again. And I suspect that Weylin has terrible plans in store. Be careful. Watch out for one another."

She approached me. I stood, my body shaking. Her hand, cool and sturdy, cupped my cheek. "You are everything I ever hoped for in a granddaughter. Fare thee well, beloved one. May the blessings of Danu shine upon you."

And then she walked out the door.

I turned to Aiden. He clasped my hands in his, raising each of mine in turn to his lips and brushing kisses across my knuckles.

"There's so much more road ahead of us," I said, swallowing. What had I thought? We'd fight a shadow-hound and be done in time for dinner, the whole ordeal over with, the world righted once more?

He seemed to understand my unspoken doubts without me having to utter them. "At least we don't travel alone."

I kissed him. "No. Not anymore."

CHAPTER TWELVE

Aiden

Vi's hand trembled in mine. The fox in me sensed trouble. One riddle might have been solved, but a dozen more revealed themselves.

The roar of my blood was in my ears. Evan. He was so close. We were so close.

Vi's hand in mine, we circled around the cottage. Like the front yard, the backyard was home to tiny faeries fluttering on wings that shone like rainbows. Birdbaths were home to splashing birds—yellow finches, red cardinals, bluebirds, pale doves. A gnome—an earth elemental—tipped his colorful cap and disappeared beneath the earth.

Vi released my hand to stand before the tall hedge, its branches an interwoven tapestry of greenery and thorns dotted with tiny, dark purple blooms. She held her hand in front of the deep green branches. "It's called faethorn. It can serve as a barrier between places—sometimes, entire worlds."

She glanced at me. Her green eyes shone brightly, a magic in them that wasn't there before. She had a sort of glow about her. Somehow, she had the bounty of autumn and the promise of spring, the fires of summer and the wisdom of winter. In that moment, I knew what the fox had known all along, since that night her magic tugged at me, a promise of wildness and magic and truth.

A promise of fates entangled and destinies revealed.

The hedge parted for us, and we stepped through. Behind us, it knitted itself back together.

"Do you think we'll ever see it again?" I wondered aloud.

"I do. I don't think Nene is done with us yet. And this sanctuary will last forever, a place for magical beings in need. But somehow, I think she's right. Whatever lies ahead of us is darkness. And Aiden..." Her voice dropped low. "I don't see how it can all be made right. I don't know if we'll all make it through this. That terrifies me."

I turned away, pretending to study the narrow dirt path ahead of us. "I came to Willow Creek to rescue Evan."

"Does that mean..."

"No!" The word came out sharp. I raked my hand through my hair. I spun to face her, taking her hand. "No. Vi, my place is in Willow Creek. My place...My place is beside you. I only meant that I'm going to fight like hell for all of you. You, Evan, Nick, Cassie. Ginny and Maeve. Every single witch and magical being in Willow Creek."

"No more stunts like the one you pulled with the shadow-hound."

I nodded absently and began to walk along the path. I wouldn't make any promises. I'd do it again to protect her, but she didn't need to hear that now.

We began to walk the narrow path between the tall, twisting trees, ducking branches and dodging briars. The woods here weren't wide and open. They were thick and full of bracken. But not evil. No, they were protective.

"Where do you think it came from? The shadow-hound?"

She gingerly stepped from one steppingstone to another as we crossed a small stream, its water shallow but swift.

"I've been thinking about that too. With everything I've learned, I'm starting to suspect Weylin conjured it to keep us from messing with the Crossroads after Cassie and Nick went there," she said after we'd both crossed.

I shivered, though the air in the woods was far from unpleasant. "So, he's boobytrapping the Crossroads now? What else do you think he has down there?"

"I don't know. Only that none of us should try it again without a lot more magical protection. Like, full magical arsenal of protection spells. The works," she said.

"Agreed."

The path twisted downward, and the trees parted, revealing a small wooden caravan wagon painted in watery hues of teal, turquoise, navy, and black. The air smelled like woodsmoke, rain, and patchouli, and beside a small fire, a man with long blond hair sat.

He sat on the ground, clad in a black t-shirt and olive-green linen pants. His long, sleek hair was pulled back in a simple ponytail. Celtic knotwork tattoos decorated his arms.

His hands lovingly cradled a guitar, one with a blue starburst and a black leather strap studded with turquoise.

He began to strum and sing, seemingly oblivious to our presence.

I recognized the song as one Cousin Ginny used to hum and sing at the fireside, on the last night of those long summer visits, "The Parting Glass." Evan's voice was hauntingly beautiful, one of those voices that could make a grown man cry if it wanted, smooth and deep with just a touch of roughness, perfectly suited for the Scottish folk song he now sang.

As he entered the song's home stretch, I raised my crooked, awkward singing voice, and joined him.

He glanced up, but his fingers didn't waver from their expert movements along the guitar's frets. His voice missed a note but picked up the next just as strong.

"Good night and joy be with you all."

As the last chord faded into silence, he set the guitar aside. "Aiden?"

"Hey, Ev." My voice was rough; the single word nearly undid me. I approached, grabbing him in a fierce bear hug. "Do you know what's happened to you?"

He shook his head. "I don't. A woman—I think she was a faerie—she told me to wait here. That I was safe. I don't know how much time has passed. I've just been waiting."

"Evan," Vi said, stepping forward. "My name is Vivienne. I'm a friend of your brother's."

Evan eyed her up and down. "What kind of friend?"

Vi blushed. "Not like that. A witch friend."

"Nick's not much for magic."

"You've been gone over a year. A lot has changed."

Evan leaned the guitar against the steps to the wagon. He seemed at peace here, like a pleasant dream. And we were about to give him a disturbing wakeup call. "I don't remember how I got here." He paused, glancing between us, his blue eyes dark like thunderheads. "I'm not sure I want to."

Vi reached into her pocket and pulled out the faerie stone. She held it out. "You have to go home, Evan. Nick is worried sick about you. Everyone is. We've come to take you home."

Evan stepped backward. Vi curled her hand around the faerie stone, frowning. I met her gaze.

Did you think it would be that easy? I asked with a furrow of my brow.

"I'm fine," Evan said, his body tensing. "Thanks for stopping by."

He strode up the steps into the wagon. I glanced at Vi. "Wait here. We just need a minute."

She nodded.

I parted the thick curtain at the back of the wagon. Inside, the quarters were simply furnished. The walls were painted with a mural of bright blue waves, swirling under a night sky. A cot in the corner reminded me of my cot in my van, only his had crisp cotton sheets in pale ivory and a silvery velvet quilt. Shelves filled with the basic necessities lined the far wall. Two floor cushions in amber orange contrasted with the blue tones. A banjo, mandolin, and small hand drum leaned in one corner.

I settled into one of the cushions. "I don't blame you for not wanting to leave. I have a place like this back...home." Did Evan even know this was the astral? I didn't want to startle him.

He snorted. "Do you? Did daddy cut you out of the will?"

"Actually, yeah. He did exactly that."

"Crap." He tugged at his ponytail. "Sorry."

I shrugged. "Best thing that ever happened to me. I have everything I need now. Magic, freedom, nature."

"A pretty girl to keep you warm at night?" He cocked an eyebrow. Ah, there was the Evan we all knew and loved.

"That too."

"So, what kind of a shifter did you turn out to be?"

"Fox."

He laughed. "I would've figured Liam for the tricksy one."

I shrugged. "He's a wolf."

He laughed harder. "Of course, he is."

I leaned in. "Evan, Nick is worried sick. I've never seen him like this. You have to come home."

"I. Can't." He gritted his teeth.

"Why not?"

A tremor wracked his body. "I can't remember. I don't *want* to remember."

"Why don't you want to?"

His eyebrows knitted together as his chest heaved a dark sigh. "I think I did something horrible. Something, maybe unforgiveable."

"Like what?" I kept my voice soft. It hadn't been his fault, but maybe he felt it was. Maybe that was the key to breaking the curse. Helping him realize what had happened — and that it hadn't been his fault.

He slammed his fist into the wall. The pots and pans on the shelf rattled at the force. "I don't know!"

"Nick loves you. You're his brother. No matter what." The words tasted bitter in my throat, but that was my baggage. Nick and Evan were different from me and Liam.

Evan narrowed his gaze. "Why do you keep talking about Nick so much? What about Gran or Mom?"

I felt the color drain from my face. I wouldn't lie, but I didn't dare speak the truth.

Evan leaned in. "Tell me."

"I..."

There was a rage in him that hadn't been there before.

"Why are you so angry, Evan?"

"Because you're lying."

"I didn't lie."

"Tricking me, then." Pain mixed with anger, a storm building in him. In this form, he was pure emotion, unrestrained. From joy to sorrow, from rage to sadness in an instant. It wasn't his fault. He couldn't ground his energy, so it just swirled and built like a storm.

"I'm not trying to trick you. I just want to remind you that your brother loves you. We all need you to come home."

"No."

"Why?"

"I can't face it." He stormed back out the door, leaving me in the wagon, dimly lit by metal lanterns that gleamed like moonlight.

When I got up to follow, I saw him storming down the path we'd entered from.

I started to go after him, but Vi grabbed my arm.

"My turn to try."

"You don't understand..."

She speared me with her gaze, her eyes fierce. "I might."

I didn't dare argue with the conviction in her voice. I let her lead the way as we followed him down the path.

Vi

Thunder rumbled overhead, seeming to shake the trees themselves. It had been cool and sunny before, but now, rain fell in sheets as we trailed after Evan.

"Evan, wait," I said, panting. Could you get winded on the astral plane? Apparently so.

After a long while, he reached the edge of the creek. Unlike where Aiden and I had crossed on the steppingstones, the water here was swift and raging. Not deep, but deep enough to sweep a person off their feet and carry them away.

He stopped and turned to look at me. In the torrential rain, his face gleamed with a terrible sadness, a pain that sent my hand flying to my neck, to my rose quartz. He followed my movement.

"You're a witch," he said, the word plain.

I nodded. "Yes." I practically had to shout to be heard over the pouring rain. I approached him slowly. I felt Aiden hanging back, waiting, but out of earshot for now. I cocked my head. "And so are you. Your coven needs you. Your family needs you. Remember who you are."

Evan clenched his fists at his side and turned toward the raging water. "I don't know what I am. I think maybe, somehow..." He trailed off. I stayed motionless, scarcely daring to breathe as I waited for him to continue. "I think I betrayed everyone I ever loved and who ever loved me. I think I betrayed everything I ever believed in."

"But you're not sure? I feel like, if you did those things, you would be sure you'd done them." I had to be careful. There was something off in Evan's aura, swirls of deep indigo and stormy gray, remnants of something left behind.

He shook his head. When he turned back to me, his blue gaze was intense, like the hottest part of the flame. Though his resemblance to his twin brother was clear, it was obvious that their personalities were night and day. "I forgot. Why would I forget?"

I swallowed and stepped forward, edging just a teensy bit closer to him. "A spell. A dark spell. You might call it a curse." I could see it now, how it clung to him like a second shadow, one that wasn't his. "I think I can help you."

"How?" The word came out a pained croak. There were memories of sadness in it, a tinge of pure anguish. What lay before Evan was a painful path. But the only way to get to dawn was to pass through the night. If we could help him end the curse, we could help him find healing.

The rain still fell steadily, but a little slower. "Let's sit."

He backed away.

"I can help you, Evan."

"Who are you? Why are you here?"

"A friend of Nick's."

"Nick doesn't have witchy friends."

"A friend of Bailee's too."

Something flickered in his gaze.

"Bailee?"

"She just moved back to Willow Creek this summer. And she misses you like crazy."

He turned away from me. "They're better off without me."

"No. They love you. And from what I hear, you're a good person. A bit of a maverick, but with an amazing heart. Aiden wouldn't have journeyed all this way if you weren't."

"You're a friend of Bailee's?"

I nodded.

"What about my Gran? My mom? You know them, then?"

"I..." I glanced at Aiden.

He stepped forward.

"They need you, Evan," Aiden said. "They all need you. We all need you. I'm sorry. I know this will hurt. But you have to remember."

Evan fell to his knees. The rain poured. Thunder shook the earth beneath us.

Aiden placed his hands on Evan's shoulders.

"Remember," I whispered, letting my magic—half-fae, half-witch, weave itself into the single word. "Remember. Remember."

Evan's scream pierced the air, as raw as the thunder, but filled with pain. When he unclenched his fists, jagged shards of mystical lightning sprang forth.

Aiden tackled me to the ground. I grunted as my shoulder hit a rock on the way down. He gazed down at me. "Are you okay?"

"Uh-huh. I'm fine."

Aiden rolled slowly off me. He stood, and I struggled to scramble to my feet. "Let's go home," Aiden said to his cousin.

But Evan didn't even look at him.

Lightning swirled around Evan's body now. His eyes continued to glow like the hottest part of a flame.

"Home? Where is home?" There was anguish—a soul torn from its world, a soul with hints of a poisonous curse in its aura.

"Where it's always been," Aiden continued. Worry etched his face, and his whole body was tense, but his voice was soft, steady. The man was not unflappable, but he could play the role. He would've made a good lawyer, after all. Steady under pressure. "Come back to Willow Creek. To the farm. To Nick. To the ones who love you."

"Gran? Mom? They're gone, aren't they?"

"Not gone. Not forever. Not if we help them. Not if we save them. But we have to stop your dad. And we need you to do that."

The lightning in Evan's aura flickered but didn't dissipate. Aiden started to approach, but then seemed to think better of it. Wise move. I wasn't sure we could die in this place, but I wasn't about to find out.

Aiden knelt on the ground. "This isn't you, Evan. Back at the camp, playing that guitar, that's you. The guy who could turn anything into a joke. A little wild, but with a big heart. That's you. You have to remember who you are."

Evan's chest fell in ragged breaths. His face contorted in a pain that wracked me in waves. I released the rose quartz that I'd unconsciously been rubbing between my fingers, letting it fall against my shirt. I stepped between them, daring to reach out and touch Evan. My hand pressed against his chest. It was the only way. The only way to break the curse.

"Look at me," I commanded gently. Our gazes locked. "You are not alone. None of us are alone. But if you shut yourself away from the ones you love, from your magic, from the world, from all the beauty and the pain, you will never truly live. I watched my grandfather live his whole life denying his magic. Don't let that be you. Don't do that to yourself. Don't do that to your family, your friends. Come home. Let yourself heal."

I unclasped the rose quartz from my neck and slid it around his. It looked a bit out of place on its dainty silver chain, but he needed it. Rose quartz: a stone of unconditional love. A stone of forgiveness. Not just for others, but for the self.

His eyes met mine. "What if I can't?"

"You can." There was a conviction in my voice. I wasn't lying. I wasn't pretending to be brave, hiding anxiety. "We all can."

"I don't know how to get back."

I reached for his hands. They were cold, like he'd been working outside on a frosty day. I clasped them in mine. The blue lightning still flickered in his aura. "The storms are you, Evan Felson. The storms are you, trying to break through. The part of you that's here, trying to get back to Willow Creek. Trying to get back home."

I tilted my head back. "Let it rain." Magic, unlike any I'd ever known, coursed through me, deep and wild, like a molten river.

"Let it rain," I called again.

"Let it rain."

Lightning, in hues of blue, purple, red, and gold, lit up the sky. There was a deafening crack. The distant sound of Aiden calling my name.

When I tumbled down, it wasn't into some abyss of darkness. I fell into a sea of mystical energy, a churning kaleidoscope of colors, a memory of magic.

I recognized it as the Crossroads, as magic waiting to be born into the world.

And I welcomed it, just as it welcomed me.

CHAPTER THIRTEEN

Vi

The air around me buzzed with magic—like ten thousand bees with their bodies buried in the most fragrant of flowers. My body gave a pleasant sigh.

The place looked like the Crossroads of Magic, but if this was the place where Aiden and I had faced the shadow-hound, it was completely transformed. The roots above me glistened, like they'd been brushed with bronze and copper. The crystals that jutted from the ceiling above glowed, casting iridescent pools of light on the earth and rocks around me. The air smelled of fresh rain and wild forests with a hint of woodsmoke and candlewax, and something vaguely citrusy—bergamot, perhaps?

I sat on a bed of moss. Vines with deep-green leaves and crimson roses formed an arch overhead. The shadows didn't feel dark and menacing like they did before. Instead, they mingled with light that didn't have a source. It was simply, it seemed, the nature of the place itself: light and shadow, moon and sun, mystery and knowing.

A massive flurry of wings drew my attention. With a soft, sad call, an owl landed before me. Our eyes locked. I bowed my head.

"You really are her familiar, aren't you? The Guardian's?"

I heard no words this time. We needed none. An understanding passed between us.

"She won't survive this, will she?"

I felt a sense of affirmation, a sense of dread, in my heart. My stomach roiled.

I pushed past the lump in my throat. "We can heal this place, wild lady. Daughter of the moon, what was broken can be healed. What was lost can be restored." It was a vow, a solemn promise—one I didn't intend to break.

Primrose.

I knitted my brows together. "That's your name?"

A soft series of hoots was her response.

I rose, dipping my head as I passed under the arch. I held out my arm and allowed her to land on me. She was lighter than I expected. Mostly, I suspected she was made of magic.

"Primrose, familiar of Nettie, the Guardian of the Crossroads of Magic, my name is Vivienne Rose Gearhart. I am a witch. I am a faerie. I don't know what exactly that means—not yet. But I'm going to fight like hell to find out."

There will be pain. There will be shadow. And rebirth will come only after the death.

And then she took flight and disappeared down the twisting caverns of the Crossroads. I suspected we'd cross paths again soon. But her warning—or perhaps, the Guardian's warning, and Primrose was only a messenger—sent my pulse racing.

The words echoed in my head.

A darting in the shadows caught my eye. A small creature moved toward me, coppery fur shimmering. My lips curled into a sad smile. I knelt down.

Time to come home.

"Home?"

Open your eyes.

"They are open," I pointed out.

Wake up.

"I..."

He was right. The Crossroads didn't look like this—maybe it did once, and maybe it would again, but it didn't. Not now. And Evan?

The memory of Evan, of the violent, multi-colored lightning tore through me.

I gasped, pitching forward.

Vi

Aiden lay beside me in my bed in my apartment. We were facing each other, our hands clasped. The plum-hued bedsheets were soft against my skin, clad in an ankle-length nightie of black silk trimmed with blush-pink lace. An ivory bedspread patterned with black roses and vines completed the look. Outside, the sky was dark with a bit of light that hinted at the in-between times. Twilight or dawn? That was the question.

I sat up.

"Careful," he said.

"How long?"

"You slept all night. It's almost dawn."

I cocked an ear. "It's quiet. No storms."

"Clear skies since we returned."

My stomach clenched. "It's not over, Aiden. Weylin, his shadowy magic. Whatever plans he has for the Crossroads." I didn't tell him what the Guardian's familiar told me. I couldn't bring myself to.

He cupped my cheeks and kissed my forehead. "I know. But Cassie came by to check on us. She said Evan is back. He's not..." He leaned back, raking his fingers through his dark hair. "It's going to be hard. He remembers what happened, how Weylin used him. But he's awake. He's talking to everyone. We did it."

I squeezed Aiden's hand. A pang of guilt made my stomach feel even more queasy. Aiden had come here for Evan, not for me. "You should go to him."

He shook his head. "Nick and Cassie are there. And Bailee. They said to call when you woke up. They all want to see you."

I nodded. "We all have a *lot* to talk about."

He kissed my lips. "We do."

Aiden slipped out from under the covers. He wore no shirt, only a pair of black pants in soft, loose cotton.

I swallowed as I watched, heat flooding my body as I remembered what we'd shared in the astral. Had it been real? Could it survive in this world, a world that was messy, where time wasn't suspended and fairytale cottages didn't let you conjure romantic boudoir scenes out of thin air?

He paused at the door. "Cassie brought some soup. I thought you might be hungry."

I shook my head. "Just thirsty." I stretched my legs, then stopped as my feet bumped into a lump. Rosemary. She opened her eyes and meowed at me. I ran my fingers through her fur. "I missed you, lovey. So much." Unable to resist, I bent forward and kissed the top of her head.

She purred even harder. She was my familiar, just as Primrose was Nettie's.

Aiden returned a few minutes later with a pot of chamomile-rosehip tea and two glasses of water on a vintage silver tray that had once belonged to Bailee's grandmother.

He sat on the edge of the bed, stroking Rosemary's fur. He handed me a glass of water, and I took a few long gulps.

"Vi?" His voice was rough.

I set the glass on the nightstand. "Yeah?"

"I'm staying in Willow Creek. And not just because of the coven or because of Evan. I..." His gaze traveled to the window. The sound of a truck on the street below cut through the silence — probably an early-morning delivery to the Thirsty Fiddler next door. "I'm staying for you. I know a lot has happened. It's okay if you don't know what you want, if you need more time. I guess, I don't know, maybe it's the fox in me, but if my instincts tell me something, I trust them. They told me to run two years ago. I don't think I ever really stopped until I got to Willow Creek. Until all that running brought me to you."

My lips curled upward. I set the tea on the nightstand, forgotten. "To me?"

He kissed one of my cheeks, then the other. "To you, sweet Vi." His voice, a low, rough rumble, sent tingles down my spine.

He began to trail kisses down my neck, then pulled away.

I moaned. I was hungry — starving. But not for food. Using all my strength, I pushed him down on the bed.

After we lay there, breathless and sated, I trailed my fingers over his chest. "I was running for a long time too. Not from someone or something. Maybe something inside of myself. My thoughts. A secret legacy I forgot. I don't know." I curled my body against his, feeling his heartbeat as it slowed to a more normal pace. "But I'm glad now. I'm glad all that running brought me to you. I think this is where I belong."

"In Willow Creek?" he asked, his voice deep and husky.

"In Willow Creek. And right here. With you."

We drifted off to sleep. When I opened my eyes, Aiden was in the kitchen, feeding Rosemary and washing blueberries to serve with Greek yogurt and honey.

We ate a quick breakfast, showered, and hopped in the car to go see Evan.

None of us was alone on our journey. Not anymore.

That's what a coven was, after all.

Just another word for family.

TANGLED MAGIC SERIES

A COVEN OF WITCHES
WITH A TANGLED DESTINY...

Welcome to Willow Creek, Virginia: A small town that's home to a coven of witches–and a mystical nexus known as the Crossroads of Magic.

One year ago, a sinister curse destroyed the coven. Now, it's up to the surviving members–including a time traveling witch from the Seventies, a fox shifter, and the local librarian–to save their coven, their town, and the Crossroads of Magic itself.

Perfect for readers who like their paranormal romance served with a side of witchcraft, tarot cards, and small-town charm.

ACKNOWLEDGEMENTS

Many thanks to so many wonderful people who helped, encouraged, and supported the creation of this book:

To my husband, Ryan, for his support of my storyteller's journey and his honest feedback on this and so many other stories. To my brother Justin for beta-reading this story and offering feedback. To Kathleen Foucart of Critiques by Katie with her expert eye, who saw the sparkle amid the dust. To Victoria Cooper of Victoria Cooper Art, for her hard work on the cover design for the Tangled Magic Series.

And to S. J. Tucker, whose lyrics appear at the opening of this story, for allowing me to include her words in *Tangled Fates*. For those who love their music with a healthy dose of magic and whimsy, I encourage you to visit her at https://www.patreon.com/join/sjtuckermusic.

And to every reader who loves magic, who believes in worlds within words, who longs for a good book, whose breath catches for a character in a book, and who longs for a happily ever after: Thank you for your relentless imagination and boundless curiosity!

There is magic in this world. Every raindrop, every sunrise, every page, every soul, and every heart.

And that magic, in all of us and in all things? It's the reason I write, the wellspring of my stories.

So, basically, if you're reading these words, thank you!

About the Author

Equal parts bookworm, flower child, and eclectic witch, Denise D. Young writes fantasy and paranormal romance featuring witches, magic, faeries, and the occasional shifter.

Whatever the flavor of the magic, it's always served with a brisk cup of tea–and the promise of romance varying from sweet to sensual.

She lives with her husband and their animals in the mountains of Virginia, where small towns and tall trees inspire her stories. She reads tarot cards, collects crystals, gazes at stars, and believes magic is the answer (no matter what the question was).

If you've ever hoped to find a book of spells in a dusty attic, if you suspect every misty forest contains a hidden portal to another realm, or if you don't mind a little darkness before your happily-ever-after, her books might be just the thing you've been waiting for.

Visit www.denisedyoungbooks.com
for excerpts, extras, and a dash of magic!

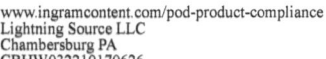